A LITTLE BIT WHISKEY

A CANDLEWOOD FALLS NOVEL

THE RIVER WINERY: NOIR'S STORY

JEN TALTY

A LITTLE BIT WHISKEY

A Candlewood Falls Novel
The River Winery Series

by
USA Today Bestselling Author
JEN TALTY

PRAISE FOR JEN TALTY

"*Deadly Secrets* is the best of romance and suspense in one hot read!" *NYT Bestselling Author Jennifer Probst*

"A charming setting and a steamy couple heat up the pages in a suspenseful story I couldn't put down!" *NY Times and USA today Bestselling Author Donna Grant*

"Jen Talty's books will grab your attention and pull you into a world of relatable characters, strong personalities, humor, and believable storylines. You'll laugh, you'll cry, and you'll rush to get the next book she releases!" Natalie Ann USA Today Bestselling Author

"I positively loved *In Two Weeks*, and highly recommend it. The writing is wonderful, the story is fantastic, and the characters will keep you coming back for more. I can't wait to get my hands on future installments of the NYS Troopers series." *Long and Short Reviews*

"*In Two Weeks* hooks the reader from page one. This is a fast paced story where the development of the romance grabs you emotionally and the suspense keeps you sitting on the edge of your chair. Great characters, great writing, and a believable plot that can be a warning to all of us." *Desiree Holt, USA Today Bestseller*

"*Dark Water* delivers an engaging portrait of wounded hearts as the memorable characters take you on a healing journey of love. A mysterious death brings danger and intrigue into the drama, while sultry passions brew into a believable plot that melts the reader's heart. Jen Talty pens an entertaining romance that grips the heart as the colorful and dangerous story unfolds into a chilling ending." *Night Owl Reviews*

"This is not the typical love story, nor is it the typical mystery. The characters are well rounded and interesting." *You Gotta Read Reviews*

"*Murder in Paradise Bay* is a fast-paced romantic thriller with plenty of twists and turns to keep you guessing until the end. You won't want to miss this one..." *USA Today bestselling author Janice Maynard*

This is a work of fiction. Names, characters, places, and incidents are the product of the author's imagination or are used fictitiously. Any resemblance to actual persons, living or dead, or actual events or locales is entirely coincidental.

A LITTLE BIT WHISKEY

Copyright © 2023 by Jen Talty

Printed in the USA

1

CARTER

C arter River raked a hand through his hair. Exhaustion settled into his bones. He set the hose on the ground. He'd been at this for two hours. Smoke continued to rise from the hotel like the tentacles of an octopus reaching for its prey. This was no way to start the month of December. This time of year was supposed to be filled with joy. Not devastation and destruction.

"Go home, Carter. You've done enough." Silas slapped him on the back. "You have a wedding in a few hours and a grandson to say goodbye to. The fire department has this covered. There isn't anything you can do now." He wiped his soot-filled hands across his coat. The pain and sorrow etched in the man's eyes dived deep into Carter's soul.

Carter had known Silas his entire life. They had been friends since they were young boys hanging out in the town center doing nothing but getting in trouble. Their bond had always been strong, even when Silas had become somewhat of a recluse living up on his mountain and Carter had married the town's crazy woman.

Neither one of those things were true, but people loved to gossip, and neither Silas nor Carter gave a fucking rat's ass. They certainly did get a few good laughs at poker over the insane rumors the good people of Candlewood Falls told about both of them. Some of them were downright hysterical. The ones that weren't, Silas and Carter generally got the last chuckle.

However, one currently weighed heavily on his mind, but that had nothing to do with Silas, and Carter wouldn't dare bring up his own troubles now.

"Are you sure? I can stay a little while longer," Carter said.

"Avoiding Weezer?" Silas laughed.

"Something like that."

"Go home, old man. And don't give me the old song and dance about the Holiday Showcase. You know we can't hold it now."

Carter glanced around at half the town. Old and young had come out to help. Most he knew well. The majority he called friends. Some he tolerated. And a few he searched for a similarity to one particular person, something he did more often than he cared to admit. "I'm just overwhelmed with this so-called small family wedding. You know Weezer. She puts her heart and soul into everything she does."

"That's why you love her." Silas smiled. "But seriously. Get your ass home."

"Call me if you need anything," Carter said. "And I mean anything. You hear me? And don't you and Claudia worry about coming to Merlot and Talbot's wedding. They will understand, considering the circumstances."

"Are you kidding me?" Silas laughed. "Claudia would put me six feet under if we missed that. Talbot is like a daughter to her and she helped raise Corbin. She's going to want to see that boy off. I can't believe he's going to be Delta Force. He's one amazing young man."

"He sure is." Carter nodded. "Weezer will send over some food."

"Not necessary."

"Doesn't matter. She was up in the kitchen when I left. You've always been there for us when things got tough. It's the least we can do."

"I'm sure that was a ruse for working on the Holiday Showcase. She's already told Claudia not to worry about a thing. She'd take all the plans Claudia had and use them. I also wouldn't put it past Weezer to be plotting how to get Noir and Tamsyn to admit they're in a relationship."

Carter cocked his head. "And what the hell would you know about that?" Carter didn't keep much from

Silas. Outside of Weezer, Silas was the one person he could tell anything to, but he didn't often give up the secrets of his children. That was where he drew the line on most days. Especially when it came to what was happening in Noir's life. He would have enough to deal with when that came to light. He didn't need his father gossiping with Silas.

"Are you going to deny it?"

"No, but I don't think those two want anyone to know, and I'm sure you can understand why."

"Any luck finding out who her father is?" Silas asked.

"That trail has been cold for a few years, but I haven't given up."

"Does Tamsyn know you're still looking?"

"She hasn't asked me about it in a while. However, I promised her I'd always keep my private investigator on retainer for it and I always keep my word."

"That you do." Silas waved to Claudia. "I best go see what she needs. That woman sure keeps me on my toes."

Carter's lips curled into a smile. It was good to see his old friend happy. Claudia had been good for him in more ways than one. "I'll see you later." Carter strolled toward where his son, Malbec, stood with his sons-in-law, Trey and Dax. "Come on. We best get going. I'm sure your mom is putting a hole in the kitchen floor by now."

"This is just terrible." Malbec, Carter's oldest son,

turned on his heel, stuffing his hands in his sweatshirt pocket, and strolled toward the parking area. "I can't believe this happened, and right before the Holiday Showcase."

"Let's not remind your mother about that. I'm sure once we get past this wedding, it's all she's going to be able to focus on. But for now, that attention needs to be on Talbot and Merlot. They deserve this day."

Trey laughed. "I'm sure that wheel is already in motion and emails sent to everyone on the showcase committee."

"It's not funny." Carter glared. "You haven't been in this family long enough to understand how crazy Weezer can get."

"I remember the year before I went away to chase my dream; she was in an all-out war with Mrs. Cummings," Dax said. "It was so bad that Chablis wanted to throw the three-legged race."

"We all did." Carter glanced over his shoulder. He hated leaving his friend like this, but Silas was right. There wasn't much Carter could do. "I was honestly so happy we weren't awarded it this year. But we have to step up to the plate. Silas and Claudia need us."

"See you at home in a few hours, Dad," Malbec said. "Call us if you need us to do or bring anything."

"Will do." Carter slipped behind the steering wheel and did his best to focus on Merlot's nuptials. That young man deserved some happiness in his life, and he was finally getting it in spades. He reached for his cell one last time.

Nothing from Noir.

He couldn't decide if that was a good thing. Or a bad thing.

Carter hated it when his kids kept secrets, but he understood this one. Not only would every single one of his siblings have something to say about it, but this town wouldn't be able to let sleeping dogs lie.

Nope. They'd bring up every single nasty rumor that had ever been told about that poor girl and her mother. Half of them weren't true, or based in half-truths. And the only two that mattered were what happened to Elizabeth and who Tamsyn's father was.

He set his cell in the holder. Noir would tell his family when he was ready. Carter could only hope it was before someone decided to make it headline news.

And unfortunately for them, it would.

Tamsyn

There were a few things in life that Tamsyn Tuttle swore would never happen, including cozying up to the River family. She'd avoided six of the seven children most of her childhood.

Zinny had been two grades behind Tamsyn, and

Pinot Noir—who went by Noir—and his twin Nebbiolo one year older. They had never been mean to her, especially Noir. He'd actually defended her on more than one occasion when the rumors about her mother would circulate. He would often find her sitting by herself. He would quietly message her, telling her he understood and that if she ever wanted to talk, he'd listen. At first, she ignored him, not trusting that he meant it.

But that soon changed, and their friendship emerged.

Things at school were compounded when the town decided to make it their business to speculate on who her father might be. One candidate had been Carter.

Even when that made the kids at school even crueler to her—and the River kids—Noir still stuck up for her.

Shortly after graduation, she learned the truth, but that had only come after she'd made a horrible accusation, one she wished she could take back. She would be forever grateful to Carter for dealing with the situation so kindly. Not because he had to, but he wanted to give her some peace of mind.

And he wanted to help.

However, he'd never been able to give her the answers she desired, but she'd never given up any part of her search and neither had Carter.

Noir rolled and stretched. "Good morning." He pulled her into his arms and gave her a quick kiss. "What time is it?"

"A little after eight." While she had always valued his friendship, never in a million years did she ever expect to wind up in his bed.

Yet, there she was, snuggled up beside him, naked.

"We better get our asses in gear." He reached for his cell.

"I don't think it's a good idea for me to crash a family wedding." Spending time with Noir in private was easy. Fun. She enjoyed every second of it. But putting their relationship on display for anyone would be a clusterfuck.

"Shit," he muttered as he tapped his screen.

She peered over his shoulder. "What's the matter?"

"I missed a family group text from my dad. There was a fire at Silas and Claudia's place." Noir threw back the covers and hiked up his boxers. He was a fine specimen of man with taut muscles, dark hair, five o'clock shadow, and bright-blue eyes. "I guess the only ones who showed up were Dax, Trey, and Malbec, so I'm not the only one in the doghouse." He cocked his head. "Speaking of dogs, I don't hear one incessantly barking, do you?"

She pulled the covers to her chin and sat up. For the last month, she'd spent most of her nights at Noir's place and every damn morning, Nebbiolo's stupid mutt woke them up at six sharp. "As a matter of fact, I don't."

"That dog walker—trainer person—has been coming every day to work with the mutt, but she

8

doesn't come until later." Noir shrugged. "Maybe my twin decided to head over to my folks' early." He held out his hand. "Come shower with me and we'll take one car."

"I have a night shift." She hugged herself. Just because she let Noir into her life, didn't mean she wanted the rest of his family, especially his mother.

Not only did she owe her one hell of an apology, but Tamsyn worried Weezer would never accept her being in Noir's life.

Their relationship—if she dared to call it that—had started as one drunken tango and turned into a few more nights of her tired of being alone with her own pathetic thoughts. She had dedicated her life to the Candlewood Falls Police Department. She'd thrown herself into her work because it gave her access to things she might not have had otherwise when it came to finding her mother.

Only at every turn, she came up empty in part thanks to the man who raised her—who also happened to be her boss.

Noir tugged at her arm. "You can take my car. Nebbiolo can drive me back here after the wedding. Or one of my other siblings can drop me off." He cocked a brow. "Or are we still hiding that we're dating from everyone?"

She groaned. Dating was such a strong word. She hadn't had a boyfriend in over two years. The last one had broken up with her because he couldn't stand being second in her life to a ghost.

His words—not hers.

"Why can't we enjoy each other in private?"

Noir sat on the edge of the bed. He rested his hand over hers, rubbing his thumb across her skin tenderly. Growing up, he and his twin had been so different from the rest of his siblings. Everyone in his family had these big personalities, much like their mother. They were loud, opinionated, and didn't care what anyone in this town thought of them.

Tamsyn didn't have that luxury. Not because she was a cop, but because of her past and all the rumors that continued to circulate through society about the disappearance of her mother and who her biological father could be. It was as if Tamsyn walked through the streets with a big scarlet letter embroidered on her shirt.

However, Noir had been a reserved soul. He was quiet all through high school. His best friend had been his twin and they did everything together, including going off to a local college. They had been roommates then and continued when they moved back. They got their first job selling liquor at the same company and they were almost never seen without the other. Their friendship circle had remained small, unlike their siblings, who managed to be somewhat popular in a town that feared their mother, whispered about their family behind their backs, and poked fun at them to their faces.

But Noir had struggled with how the world perceived him and it drove him to retreat. On and off through her youth, she and Noir had been *friendly*. He'd always been kind to her, when other kids were cruel. She appreciated his tender soul, but resented he'd been the only one who came to her defense.

"We've been doing this for over a month now," Noir said. "I'm tired of hiding out. Of having takeout in my place or yours. I want to be able to take you out to a restaurant. I don't understand why you care what anyone might have to say about us dating."

"Seriously? You have to ask me that question? You know the rumor as well as I do." She covered his mouth. "And don't tell me that people have forgotten, because they haven't. It might not be the first thought that comes to mind when people see me. But it's there. Lurking in the shadows."

He batted her hand away. "You're being dramatic."

"Am I?" She glared. "We're coming up on the anniversary of my mom's disappearance and every year our local news brings it up. It's made worse that our resident newscaster is planning on doing a series on my mother."

"I don't pay any attention to her and you shouldn't either," Noir said. "She's a gossip and would toss her own family under the bus if she thought it would make her relevant."

"Hard to ignore when she's showing up at the station and my house, asking for an interview, and both Fred and Anna are considering granting her one."

"I can almost understand Anna doing it, but Fred? He's always been a facts first kind of cop."

"True. And he's the one who's constantly trying to get me to stop what he calls an obsession." Tamsyn hid so much from Fred. She had a file five inches thick regarding her mom and the list of potential men who could be her father, but at the end of the day, all it gave her was a dead end and one big fat fucking headache. "But when it comes to Anna, he will go along to keep the peace with his wife."

"I don't understand why she's so concerned with it all. It doesn't affect her, only you."

"And it could bring some ugly rumors back to your family."

"None of which are true. I knew that before you showed me the proof."

"Anna doesn't like anyone in your family, especially Weezer." Tamsyn pursed her lips. "That could be her motivation. It wouldn't be the first time she's tried to make your mom look bad. One more reason I should stay away."

"You're making excuses." Noir stood, releasing her hand. He glared. "If all you want is a roll in the hay every once in a while, then say it. If that's all we are, then maybe this has run its course. I need to shower and go to my brother's wedding. I care about you and want you there—as my girlfriend—but if that's not what you want, fine. But I'm not going to keep doing this. I want more. If you do too, come to the wedding." He turned on his heel and stormed out of the bedroom.

Shit.

Noir had been the best thing that had happened to her in years. It had been unexpected. Every time they got together, she worried it would be the last. And yet, she was the one who couldn't take the next step. The only person who knew about them had been Nebbiolo, and he wouldn't tell anyone because that man barely spoke. He was quieter than Noir, and that was hard to do.

Was she really worried about the rumor mill?

Or what Anna was going to say about her dating Noir River?

She shivered.

Anna and Fred had raised her from the age of ten, when her mother had disappeared. Anna had her own brand of distaste for the River family and she had made it clear that Tamsyn was to keep her distance. That hadn't been easy to do. She'd been drawn to Noir at an early age, but their quiet friendship remained on the fringe. Their conversations through middle and high school were kept private through messaging apps or hidden under the football stands. They didn't speak often. It was only out of necessity when the rumors reared their ugly heads. Or when the kids were unusually mean.

But no matter what, Noir had always been there for her when she needed a friend the most. He never judged her or made her feel that her need for answers was crazy.

"Fuck it." Tamsyn tossed back the comforter and reached for a towel. She wrapped it around her body and raced down the hallway, pushing open the bathroom door, but Noir wasn't in there. "Noir? Where are you?"

"In the kitchen," he said.

"Is Nebbiolo out there?"

"Nope."

Securing the towel, she inched into the small galley kitchen.

Noir leaned against the sink holding a piece of paper. "You're not going to believe this one."

"What's going on?"

"My fucking twin ran off with the dog trainer lady." Noir lifted his gaze. "They got married yesterday. Nebbiolo says they will be back in time for Merlot's wedding." He raked a hand through his hair. "I can't believe he did this without at least me."

"Weezer is going to fucking kill him and then maybe June, although I kind of like her and you have to admit, she's good for your twin."

"Good for him or not, getting married before my folks even officially met her isn't smart."

Tamsyn's memories of her mother were few and far between, but one had stuck to her brain like superglue.

She couldn't shake it if she tried and right now, it played through her mind like a bad horror movie.

She and her mom had gone to town after supper for some ice cream, and Weezer had stopped them in the middle of the sidewalk. Her mother had her sit on the park bench a few feet away, but Tamsyn had heard and seen the fight.

Stay away from my husband and my family. You've caused enough damage. We all know the truth and you perpetuating the lie is hurting the people I love the most in this world. Stop it, or you will live to regret it.

Weezer's words reached deep into her soul to this day. They wrapped around her heart, sucking the life out of her slowly, making it hard to breathe.

Her mom disappeared two days later.

Noir crumpled the paper and tossed it in the trash. "He expects me to tell my folks in case he's late. I can't believe that asshole. He knows how my mom gets when she's left out of big things in her kids' lives, not to mention, she'll take it out on me. Blame me for letting him run off and get married to a woman he's only known for a few weeks. And to someone she hasn't even met yet. This is going to suck."

"If ever there was a time for me not to come to a family event, this would be it." Tamsyn ran her fingers across Noir's shoulder. "But I'll go. For you. As moral support. As your girlfriend," she whispered, nearly choking on the last word. Caring for Noir came easy. He was kind, considerate, and put up with all her rules.

Being his official girlfriend would be hard as hell, though.

Carter had never taken to the streets with the proof. He didn't feel the need. He'd told her that if she wanted to, that was her call. He'd back her decision no matter what. So would his wife and the rest of the family. The only reason she hadn't was it would open up a whole lot of speculation and gossip that she didn't want to hear.

"That wasn't very enthusiastic." He chuckled, wrapping his arm around her body. "What changed your mind? This letter or me?"

"You," she said. "What Nebbiolo did has nothing to do with it. That should make me run for the hills."

"Merlot's going to rip him a new one if he doesn't show. He and Talbot have waited a lifetime to be together. They deserve to have the whole family together for this."

"You two have never really gotten along great with him. Why is that?" The River family dynamics had been difficult to understand, and she'd tried. While her friendship with Noir over the years had been mostly one-sided, dealing with her issues, she did occasionally listen to his problems. However, because she'd never been close to any of them, all she had to go on was rumors, unearthed secrets, observation, and her cop instinct.

Those four things were incredibly contradicting.

The rumors and unearthed secrets made the River

family look like a bunch of criminals and liars. But as each rumor was debunked, and each secret revealed, it turned out the Rivers were victims of circumstance, something she could relate to.

Her observations and cop instincts told her that they were just another dysfunctional family that loved each other and would do anything to protect their own. That deep down, they were good people with good intentions, but had a wacky matriarch that often did things ass-backward, which didn't make her look good and often affected her children and husband negatively.

"Nebbiolo and I have always been the black sheep of the family. While everyone else wanted to be part of the family business, even when it was going to hell in a hand basket, we wanted nothing to do with it."

"But you're working full-time there now," she said.

He laughed. "Things are very different now that the truth of how we got the winery from Eliza Jane's family is out in the open. That really affected my folks. It almost destroyed their relationship. Their business. Everything."

"I still don't get it. I mean, Merlot didn't work for the family business. He was a parole officer for years before he came back."

"That's true, but when Malbec and Chablis quit, he felt abandoned. And my mom wouldn't trust him without his older brother and sister. Nebbiolo and I might have been young at the time, but we saw it all, heard it all, and we wanted nothing to do with it, so we carved our own path and Merlot didn't like it. He wanted us here to protect Zinny and help Mom. We walked away, and he felt like we took Zinny with us, leaving Mom high and dry. That's not what happened, and we've since cleared the air, but sometimes Merlot has a hard time letting go of things. He likes to run the winery his way. We butt heads a lot. However, we're working it out. This will put us back a little, and it pisses me off that my twin is leaving me holding the bag. He's been a selfish prick lately."

"I'm sure everyone will understand that you had nothing to do with your brother's actions," she said.

Noir let out a dry laugh. "You don't know my family. They look at me and my twin as one person sometimes. Like we share the same brain. He and I have always done everything together. But these last few months, we couldn't be further apart. My twin has been making me crazy. I don't want to live with him anymore, especially since he got that dog."

"The only reason he got Sasha was because he thought June was hot." Tamsyn took a step back and opened her towel, exposing her naked body.

Noir's eyes grew wide and a slow smile spread across his face.

"Come on. We're going to be late if we don't go shower," she said.

"You don't have to ask me twice."

Tamsyn dropped the terrycloth and raced off down the hallway with her heart beating like a hammer in her chest. She could admit to herself that she cared deeply for Noir. Being with him—privately—had been easy. Natural. They laughed at all the same things. Their conversations weren't clunky or awkward. The silent moments weren't deafening. There wasn't anything about him she didn't like.

However, being with him in public would undoubtedly bring an earthquake that would shake this town like it had never been rocked before.

2
NOIR

Noir held Tamsyn's hand as he approached the front porch of the River family home. It was nestled on the side of the winery near the river that snaked through the vineyards. The house was over a hundred years old and stood tall, overlooking the winery that his family had nourished for years.

This was his legacy and he'd learned to cherish it.

However, during his youth it had been his nightmare.

Growing up, he'd been called a bastard child since his parents had been divorced when he'd been born. That word had stung more than he cared to admit. It had helped define his personality. His older siblings had constantly told him to ignore it. To laugh it off because it didn't matter.

His parents loved him, and so did his brothers and sisters.

They were a family and no one could take that away, a concept that he felt deep in his core.

But still, the stares, the whispers, the rumors, and the name-calling stuck to his heart and soul. Nothing could erase that.

And then there had been Tamsyn's mother.

That one had pushed him over the edge. He'd only been twelve when Elizabeth Tuttle had disappeared. Even younger when the rumor mill had begun regarding Tamsyn's possible connection to his family. His parents did what they always did when it came gossip—they ignored it. But that did nothing to stop the relentless teasing that Noir and his twin suffered at the hands of other kids at school. The rest of his siblings, including his baby sister, handled it by either pushing back or brushing it off, going about the business of being popular. However, the twins weren't afforded that luxury. Tamsyn was too close in age.

It was made more complicated by Noir's growing feelings for Tamsyn.

Something he'd been trying to deny most of his life.

"Hey. Are you okay?" Tamsyn asked.

He glanced in her direction, realizing he'd paused at the base of the porch. "Just collecting my thoughts," he said. "I had been hoping Nebbiolo would have been here, but I don't see his car."

"If we stand out here much longer, it will be me getting cold feet."

"Zinny and Toby are here. So are Dax and Chablis. You'll be safe with them while I chat with my folks."

"I don't know about that," Tamsyn said. "While your siblings are always respectful of my uniform and kind when they see me, I'm not sure they like me. Not even Zinny."

"That's not true," he said. Although he had no idea how anyone felt about Tamsyn in his family. Over the years, she'd gone and made some wild accusations about his mother all based off one fight she'd witnessed as a child. Half the town had seen that fight and they'd all gotten it wrong.

It was compounded by the way Tamsyn tended to avoid his family. She was a whiskey girl, so she didn't purchase much wine. If she did, it wasn't from his family's winery. She rarely attended functions at the vineyard. When she did, it was because she was there in uniform, working officially, as security.

He squared his shoulders and made his way up the steps, a little surprised his mom wasn't there to greet him. He pushed open the door.

Dax paced in the family room with his newborn in his arms, while Chablis sat on the floor, playing with River.

TJ jumped from his seat on the sofa. "Uncle Noir." He raced across the room. "I scored the winning goal yesterday." The boy had grown at least three inches in the last year and stood close to five foot ten. He was

22

scrawny, but his muscles would soon fill out, just like his father.

"That's awesome, kid." He pounded TJ's fist. "Sorry I wasn't there to see it."

Zinny waved from the rocking chair. She held one of the latest additions to the family, her little girl, Crystal. The baby smiled and giggled at the sight of her uncle.

His siblings were pumping out babies left and right. He couldn't be happier for them. He loved his nieces and nephews. They brought everyone enormous joy, including him.

"Hey, Noir. Hi, Tamsyn," Zinny said as if having Tamsyn on his arm was a normal thing. "Nice to see you and not when you're writing me a parking ticket."

Tamsyn laughed. "You're never going to forget that, are you?"

"Nope," Zinny said. "Neither is my husband. He's still pissed at you over that one."

"I most certainly am not. She's not the one who illegally parked. You are." Toby strolled across the room, stretching out his arm. "Where's your twin?"

Noir shook Toby's hand. "I'll explain later. Where are my folks?"

"In the kitchen," Toby said.

"I'll be back in a few." He kissed Tamsyn's cheek. "I expect all of you to be nice to my date."

"Date?" Chablis asked. "Oh no, little brother. You don't get to toss that word around and then ditch. You have to explain a little more." She handed a toy to River before standing, smoothing down her slacks. "Sorry, Tamsyn. Nothing personal here, but Noir hasn't brought a date to any family function ever, and while I have nothing against him bringing you, you have to understand why it might raise a few eyebrows. I want to know what exactly is going on. When did this happen? How long have you been dating? And are you prepared for the—"

"Chablis, that's enough." Noir inched closer. It had taken him a long time to gain his voice with his older siblings. He rarely gave any of them a hard time about anything, unless it was winery business. But he wasn't going to stand there and have his girlfriend be given the third degree.

"I'm just asking for clarification." Chablis raised her hands. "It's not like we all haven't been talking about this for the last month, wondering when you two were going to come clean."

"Excuse me?" Tamsyn said.

"What my sister means, but isn't saying very well, is that it's about time the two of you are out in the open," Zinny said. "We all know. She's just giving him a hard time about keeping it a secret. As if we'd all care he's dating you, because we don't."

"If you don't care, then don't hassle us. We'll get enough shit from people in town. We don't need it from family." Noir glared at his sisters. "I'm serious."

"Relax," Chablis said. "I'm sorry if I offended you, Tamsyn. That wasn't about you. Just harassing my little brother a little for keeping secrets about his dating life. That never goes over well in this family and my little brother tends to be aloof, even with us."

"I'm not aloof. I'm private. There's a difference," he said.

Toby laughed. "Of all the siblings, you and Nebbiolo are the hardest to get to know."

"I have to second that one, and I've known you your entire life." Dax lowered his chin. "Personally, I think you two make for a nice couple and I'll do my best to keep my wife from giving you a hard time." He smiled. "Maybe you guys could come over for dinner one night. That would be nice."

"I'd like that." Chablis inched closer. She rested her hand on Tamsyn's forearm. "Winning over Noir's siblings will be easy, but our mother will be hard."

"I owe her a pretty big apology," Tamsyn said. "But today probably isn't the time to do that."

"I disagree." Zinny patted Crystal's back. "Knowing my mom, she'll demand it if you want to stay for the wedding."

"There's a bigger issue that's going to piss off Mother. It's going to send both her and Dad through the roof. Wait until you hear the yelling that's going to come from our mom's mouth when I go into that kitchen," Noir muttered. "No more razzing my girlfriend while I'm gone, got it?"

"You're seriously going to drop that teaser and leave us hanging?" Dax asked.

"Trust me, you'll hear it all soon enough." Noir sucked in a deep breath and made his way down the short hallway to the kitchen where he found his father leaning against the sink, drinking a cup of coffee. His mother sat at the table in front of her laptop and a notebook.

"Look at what the cat dragged in," his father said.

His mom didn't even lift her head.

That couldn't be a good sign.

"Sorry I didn't come help at Silas and Claudia's place this morning. I didn't see the text until later." He reached for a mug and poured a cup of steaming brew. His dad always made the best. It was strange because it was just regular coffee, but it tasted better than anyone else's.

"Really wasn't much any of us could do," his dad said.

"I feel bad for Claudia." His mom peered over her screen. "It's going to put her grand opening back and it means the Holiday Showcase won't be held there." His mother smiled. "Looks like I'm going to have to step up to the plate."

"She's been working on that all morning." His dad rolled his eyes. "Nothing I say or do will stop her now. Not even your brother's wedding." He glanced at his watch. "Which is supposed to start in less than two hours, but everyone seems to be running late, including the bride and groom."

"Until everyone gets here, I'm going to work on the

showcase." His mother adjusted her reading glasses. "Mrs. Cummings is already putting her two cents in, but if *that woman* thinks she can muscle her way into *my showcase*, she's got another thing coming."

"Toss Mrs. Cummings a bone," his father said. "If you don't, she'll be up your ass—and mine—until next year."

"No way. Give her an inch, and she'll try to take a mile." His mother shuffled some papers. When his mom got like this, there was no reasoning with her or trying to talk her into anything.

Shit. Telling his folks now about Nebbiolo running off, or that he was dating Tamsyn, would cause a shock wave that would send his mother to the moon and back.

But he had no choice. It had to be done.

"Mom, can you put that stuff away for a few minutes? I need to talk with you and Dad. It's important."

His mother lowered her chin and peered over her glasses. She glanced between his dad and back to him before closing her laptop. "That sounds ominous."

"It kind of is," he admitted, raking his fingers through his hair. "I'm not sure where to start. There are two pieces of information that I'm not sure how either of you are going to take. One involves me, the other, my twin."

"Which one is worse?" His father set his mug to the side and folded his arms.

"I'd say Nebbiolo." Noir pulled out a chair and sat across from his mother. He took a long slow sip of coffee, letting the scalding liquid fill his belly. "Dad, you might want to sit down for this one."

"I think I'll stand," his father said. "Your twin has been acting like a jerk for the last few weeks. He's been late to work and giving Zinny and Merlot a hard time."

"Whatever it is has been affecting you as well." His mother pushed her work to the side. She rarely would ever give him her full attention when the showcase was her event. She lived for that stupid thing. "You've been covering for him and don't pretend you haven't. We've all seen it."

"He's been seeing someone and it's gotten serious," Noir said.

His father laughed. "Tell us something we don't know."

"He ran off and got married." Noir held his father's gaze.

His dad's eyes widened, then narrowed. His lips parted. "When?"

"Yesterday," Noir admitted. "He left me a note stating he might be late and asked me to—"

"That little shit," his mom mumbled. "I'm going to take him and that damned dog walker—"

"She's a dog trainer and her name is June Parker." Noir had no idea why he felt the need to correct his mom, but when it came to Nebbiolo, it was what he did.

"I know who she is," his mother said. "And we've known for weeks they have been seeing each other. I also don't really care that they got married. Only that they had no respect for Merlot and Talbot. Those two had their entire lives ripped from them." His mom took a napkin from the center of the table and dabbed her eyes. "I'm going to wring your twin's neck when I see him. He had no right. They could have waited a few days. A week. Or better yet, let us throw them a wedding. He's being a selfish little asshole, as usual, and I'm sorry he put you in a position to have to tell us."

Noir stared at his mom. That was not the response he expected. Not only did he figure his parents had no idea about June, but he thought he'd covered better for his twin at the winery. Their job didn't require them to be in house every day. They traveled more, to sell the wine to restaurants, hotels, and distributors. That was their job. Nebbiolo had been so busy playing house with his new girlfriend that he'd left most of the work to Noir.

Who also had a secret girlfriend.

But Tamsyn worked sixty hours a week most of the time. She didn't demand that Noir spend every waking second in her presence.

"You shouldn't be covering for him either," his father said. "You two are too old for that shit."

"Tell me about it," Noir said. "I'm tired of it and I'll deal with it. I'm not going to live with him and his new wife. Now I have to go find a new apartment because he wants ours."

"It's about time the two of you have separate lives." His father nodded. "Why don't you move into the cottage. No one is living there now. It's yours if you want it. You can move in anytime."

"Really? Because I'll start moving in tonight," Noir said.

"Your father wouldn't have offered if we didn't mean it." His mom smiled. "It would be nice to have you closer."

"Now, you mentioned there was something else. What's going on with you, son?"

God. Noir hated it when his dad used the word *son*. It either meant his dad thought he knew something, did know something, or was pissed about something. None of which was good for Noir.

"I brought a date to the wedding," Noir admitted.

His mother smiled. "I'm not surprised."

"Tamsyn, I take it," his father stated as fact, not a question.

Noir opened his mouth, but no words tumbled from his lips. He cleared his throat and tried again. "Why would you immediately go to Tamsyn Tuttle?"

"Because you've been in love with her since the eighth grade." His father laughed.

"Did you really think we didn't know about you and Tamsyn?" his mother asked. "She's come into the winery three times in the last two weeks. She never buys wine from us. That girl has always been a little bit whiskey. Now she's buying cases and cheese boards to go with it?"

"Not to mention we saw the two of you buying takeout," his father said. "We've been patiently waiting for you to tell us. It hasn't been easy to bite our tongues."

"Just please tell me you didn't run off and get married too." His mother leaned back and gave him that funny look with her crinkled nose and crooked smile. It was meant as a teasing look, but he hated it nonetheless.

"Of course not," he said. "It's not that serious. But I'm a little shocked that you're not pissed."

"Well, that child does owe me an apology." His mother cocked her head. "She did all but accuse me of murdering her mother."

"Weezer, she was a nineteen-year-old kid when she did that. She didn't mean it. Besides, you gave everyone in this town an eyeful when you threatened Elizabeth."

"For good reason." His mother pressed her hands on the table and rose. "My darling husband, I know I promised you to keep my mouth closed all these years, but now that Tamsyn is dating our son, and she knows the truth about you, she should know some other cold hard facts about her mother."

"She's heard all the horrible things this town has had to say about Elizabeth," Noir said. "Just because her mom wasn't a pillar of society, doesn't give people the right to disparage her."

"Some of those things are true," his mom said in a soft tone.

The sound of feet shuffling into the kitchen caught Noir's attention. He turned his head. Tamsyn stood in the doorway.

Tamsyn

"I'm sorry. I didn't mean to eavesdrop." Tamsyn stood in the doorway. "But since I heard some of that, I feel as though I should address it." Her heart hammered in her throat. She'd been standing there for what seemed like an eternity, listening to Carter and Weezer talk about her, her mother, and the horrible situation that had plagued her life.

Noir raced to her side, taking her hand. "No. We shouldn't have been talking about you and your mom like that." He kissed her cheek. His soft lips brought some comfort, but not enough to erase the pain of the past.

"It's okay. We knew this all would come up the second I walked into your parents' home," Tamsyn said. "I know my mother suffered from a mental illness. My memories of her might be limited, but I lived with her and I remember certain things, like the men that came in and out of our home. The drinking. The drugs. She wasn't the best mom, but she was the only one I had. The only parent I had." Tamsyn raised her hand. "I understand that what she did to Carter was wrong and maybe I should have used the paternity test to put an end to all speculation of whether or not Carter was my father."

"That was always up to you," Carter said. "We know the truth and that's all that matters."

"But it's not fair to you that I've allowed people to keep talking about it simply because there isn't any other man in this town who ever showed my mother kindness." Tamsyn leaned into Noir's strong frame for support. "If Noir and I are going to go public, we'll need to put an end to that. And I am truly sorry for my accusation. I was acting out and I had no right. However, my mother wasn't a bad person. She made mistakes, no doubt, but just because she was a drug addict and mentally ill, that shouldn't be used against her."

"I don't disagree with that." Weezer strolled across the room and took Tamsyn's hands.

In all the years Tamsyn had known Weezer, she'd found the woman to be a contradiction. She'd seen her be kind and warm. Generous even. But cross her, and you made an enemy for life.

Tamsyn believed she'd always been somewhere in the middle.

"Your mom was a few years younger than me, but in our youth, we were friendly. I genuinely liked her, and Carter and I tried to help her as best we could. I'm so sorry that you had to witness those harsh words. While they had everything to do with her claiming to everyone in town that Carter was your father, my anger had more to do with my hurt feelings. I felt betrayed. We'd given her money. We'd done everything including offering to help with you, but she tossed that in our faces. I'd had it and I lost my temper. But what you need to understand is that your mom wouldn't give up when it came to Carter."

"Don't do this now, Weezer." Carter took a step forward.

"I want to hear this," Tamsyn said.

"Me too." Noir nodded. "I thought we were done with secrets."

"It's not a big bad dark cloud," Weezer said. "It's just something we've kept to ourselves in part because it could have caused Tamsyn more grief." She glanced over her shoulder.

Carter lifted his mug. "I should have told you when we did the paternity test and I can't believe Fred hasn't shown you the note."

"There's a note?" Tamsyn asked, releasing his mom's hands and grabbing his. "About what?" Fred had sworn he'd given her everything. Shared with her all that he knew, both personally and professionally.

Why would he keep this a secret? From her of all people. All she wanted was two answers.

Who was her father?

And what happened to her mom?

Fred had been her biggest supporter. He'd been there for her when no one else hadn't. While he didn't agree with this ongoing search, he did support her emotionally.

"The day after my big blowout with Elizabeth, she sent Carter and me a letter. She told us that she expected Carter and me to raise Tamsyn. She was adamant that you were his kid, even though that was impossible. There wasn't anything threatening about the note. Just an expectation to do the right thing. We ignored it, but the next day she was gone. Carter and I thought long and hard about taking you in, but before we even had a chance to say yes or no, Fred and Anna stepped up."

"Anna and Fred have always held that no one else wanted me." Tamsyn fought the tears that struggled to break free. "That if they didn't take me in, I would have gone to an orphanage." She cringed at the word. That had been the way Anna put it. Not Fred. He'd been a little more diplomatic and kind about the situation.

"That's not true," Carter said. "Weezer and I wouldn't have allowed that. We would have taken you in, no questions asked."

"Even with the rumors?" Tamsyn couldn't believe her ears. None of this made sense. "Why would you? I

35

mean no disrespect, but I can almost understand why Carter would. But you, Weezer?"

"I'm so misunderstood." Weezer smiled. "You were a child. You shouldn't have to pay for the sins of your parents. Our only concern and why we thought about it for a night had been you and our children. I don't hold what your mother did against you." She waved her finger. "Though, I will say, I didn't like being accused of having anything to do with your mom's disappearance, especially when I do hold myself responsible. I can't help but wonder if my words could have been the catalyst for that."

This certainly was a strange twist of events. Tamsyn sucked in a shallow breath, trying to pull her cop instincts to the forefront, but all she had was the hurt, scared, ten-year-old little girl.

"You honestly thought about taking her in?" Noir asked.

"Of course we did, son," Carter said. "We felt responsible for what happened. I also had words with Elizabeth. It had been hard for us to differentiate her mental illness and her cruelty. She had this town believing I had stepped out on my wife. It was made worse by the fact we weren't actually married or living together at the time, but we were still in a committed relationship. I took what she did to heart and a few days later, she was gone. As Tamsyn well knows, there have been no clues, except one."

"Her car being left at the train station two towns

over," Tamsyn muttered. "The trail has been as cold as ice since." She glanced at her watch. "Is it too soon to start drinking?"

Carter chuckled. "We have mimosas, if you'd like one."

The knock at the back door startled her, making her jump.

"I wonder who that could be." Carter strolled across the room. "It's Anna."

"What on earth is she doing here?" The last person Tamsyn wanted to see right about now was the woman who helped raise her. It wasn't that Tamsyn didn't like Anna, she did. But Anna cared more about appearances than she did anything else. She wanted everyone to believe they were one big happy family, but they weren't.

Anna and Fred had never legally adopted her, even though Fred had said he wanted to.

They had told Tamsyn that it would be hard to adopt because her mother was missing, not dead. And Elizabeth had never been declared dead, something Tamsyn wasn't willing to pursue.

Besides, Tamsyn didn't want a new mom. And Fred wasn't her father.

At least not biologically.

According to Anna and Fred, they couldn't have children.

And of all the men in Candlewood Falls, Fred had never once been linked to her mother, so she had quickly crossed him off her list. But during the last twenty years, he'd been the closest thing she'd ever had to a father. Their relationship was slightly distant, but that was on Tamsyn, not Fred. And Tamsyn blamed it all on Anna.

"Let's find out." Carter pulled open the door. "Hello, Anna. What brings you by?"

"I need to speak with Weezer about the email she sent about the showcase." She shifted her gaze, glaring at Weezer. "I can't believe you thought it was appropriate to… Tamsyn?" Anna paused in the middle of the kitchen and blinked. "Is something wrong? Why are you here?" She glanced down at Tamsyn's hand, which was intertwined with Noir's. "And with him?"

"She's here for Merlot and Talbot's wedding," Weezer said before Tamsyn could form any words.

"Oh. I forgot that was today." Anna adjusted her oversized purse, clutching it tightly. "Isn't that a private family gathering? Why would Tamsyn be included?" she asked with dripping disdain.

Weezer looped her arm through Tamsyn's. "She's here as—"

"Noir invited me." Tamsyn didn't want to get into her relationship status with Anna while standing in the River family home. Not when tensions were this high. "Anna, let me walk you to your car. This isn't the time to have this conversation with Weezer. Perhaps Weezer can make time in her schedule tomorrow or the next day to discuss your concerns about the showcase."

"As I stated in my email, there will be a committee meeting tomorrow at noon," Weezer said.

"You're notorious for changing the committee, so some of us are concerned we'll be replaced," Anna said. "You better not do that. It's bad enough that the fire at Claudia's place wasn't even out before you took over. You didn't even give anyone a chance to discuss possible alternatives."

"This late in the game, there isn't anyone else who could pull this thing together." Weezer glided across the kitchen like she was floating on air. She waved her hand over all the papers on the table. "I didn't simply take over. I was asked to step in by the person who was supposed to hold the showcase. I accepted."

"I believe it's more like you swooped in and offered before anyone else could." Anna waved her finger. "You are as underhanded as they come, Weezer River. Someday you'll get what you deserve and I'm going to enjoy watching it happen."

"It's time for you to leave," Weezer said.

Tamsyn curled her fingers around Anna's forearm. "Come on. Let's go." She guided Anna through the back door, glancing once over her shoulder.

Noir smiled weakly.

Carter wrapped his arm around Weezer, who looked as though she wanted to follow Anna right out to her car and give her a few more choice words.

Tamsyn couldn't blame Weezer. Anna had come in

hot. She didn't like Weezer and had made that perfectly clear over and over again.

"I'm so glad you decided to leave with me." Anna yanked open the driver's side door. "That woman thinks she owns this town. Well, I've got news for her. She doesn't and half the people on that committee don't want her to have the showcase."

That wasn't true. The only people who didn't want that to happen were Anna and Mrs. Cummings. Everyone else knew that Weezer would put on a good show. She always did. It didn't matter how Weezer got the showcase, because she cheated half the time, but every year the Holiday Showcase was at the winery, it was an event to remember.

"I'm not leaving," Tamsyn said. "Noir is my friend and I'm here to support him."

"Friend? How can you be friends with him? No one in that family has ever been kind to you. Or me. You can't trust them."

"What is your problem with Weezer?" Tamsyn had asked this question before, and the only answer she'd gotten had been there was unresolved history from childhood. Things in the past that didn't concern her, but Anna could never forgive, nor forget.

Fred, of course, went along with Anna's insane hatred for Weezer and the River family because he loved his wife. He'd shrug his shoulders and say, *Weezer is a hard nut. Carter's not a bad man, but he sides with Weezer at every turn. Things were said. Anna got hurt. I need to be there for my wife. It's as simple as that.*

However, nothing was simple because Tamsyn didn't understand. At first, she believed Anna's anger came out of what happened between Weezer and Tamsyn's mother. She'd been told that for the first few years she'd lived with Anna and Fred.

As she got older, she learned there was a whole lot more to that story, but no one ever told her the details.

If she had a chance in hell of making her relationship work with Noir, she needed that intel.

"Are you kidding me? You honestly have to ask me that question? Weezer is the reason your mother—"

"No," Tamsyn said. "That would be my problem with her and I'm over it. I want to know why you're holding a grudge. I need to know because I care about Noir. A lot."

"What the hell does that mean?" Anna jerked her head. Her eyes grew wide with shock and recognition. "No. No. No." She shook her head wildly. "You can't have feelings for that young man. It's impossible." She leaned closer. "Your mother had an affair with Carter. You know the rumors. What if they're true?"

"Oh my God. Carter would never and you know it, and I have the proof." Tamsyn should have told Fred and Anna the truth the moment she found out. She should have told the entire town. Just because the River family didn't care, didn't mean she didn't. Or anyone else.

"Proof?" Anna whispered.

"Yeah. We took a paternity test a few years ago. I should have told you. Carter left it up to me to do whatever I wanted with the information. He and Weezer didn't want to make a big deal about it, so I didn't either. The rumors had died down and other than you and Mrs. Cummings, most people accepted that Carter—"

"He and Weezer could have easily forged that document. Carter went to great lengths to make sure the love of Merlot's life appeared to be dead for twenty-one years. Carter has the means to do anything he wants."

"Oh, please. They wouldn't let me date their son if there was any chance I could be related to him." Tamsyn couldn't believe her ears. Anna was a lot of things. A gossip. A pot stirrer. A social climber. A wannabe. She had a desire to be the center of attention. A need to be the most important person in the room. She believed being married to the police chief gave her the power to run the town. Only it didn't.

"Dating?" Anna fanned herself. "Wait until your father hears this one."

"Fred is not my father," Tamsyn corrected Anna. It wasn't meant to be mean or hurtful. Just fact. She'd never once called either one of them her parents. They were the people who raised her—and she truly adored Fred—but neither one of them were her mom or dad.

Anna had asked her on multiple occasions to call

her mom, but the word could never roll off Tamsyn's tongue.

It wasn't that Tamsyn didn't love or care about Anna, she did. Anna had been kind, warm, loving even toward Tamsyn growing up. But Anna lacked that maternal instinct that Tamsyn craved. Anna was more of a warm body that tucked her in at night than a stand-in for a mother. Anna went through the motions but lacked any real emotion. She'd sit and listen to Tamsyn when she'd come home from school with a problem, but Anna couldn't provide that unconditional love a parent could. She cared more about what people thought than what was right.

Fred did better. He offered love, support, and companionship. He did more than go through the motions, but Tamsyn never truly let him completely in. At first, it was because she had this fairy-tale idea that her father would roll in on a Harley and whisk her away. But because Fred constantly asked her to stop the search, to give up on finding both her parents, and consistently taking Anna's side on everything, Tamsyn couldn't open her heart wholly.

"What is your beef with Weezer?" Tamsyn asked.

"Come home with me and I'll tell you," Anna said, glaring.

This obviously was going nowhere. "I'm staying for the wedding, but this conversation isn't over. I want an answer because I'm not going to stop seeing Noir."

"We'll see about that." Anna slipped behind the

steering wheel. "I know you have the night shift. But I expect to see you for a family dinner tomorrow night. We'll talk then." She tugged the door closed and the engine roared to life.

Tamsyn took a step back and watched Anna drive off. She glanced over her shoulder.

Noir jogged down the steps. "Are you okay?"

"Not really."

He wrapped his arms around her, pulling her into his chest. "Want to talk about it?"

"No." She rested her head on his shoulder. "Do you think your mom would tell me what happened between them in the past?"

"She might, if you asked her," Noir said. "But I'd wait until after the wedding. Merlot and Talbot are here. So is Nebbiolo and June and everyone else. It's time to get my brother married."

She glanced up. "I'm glad we're out in the open, but we're going to be the talk of this town, and that is going to be hell."

3

TAMSYN

Tamsyn took the glass of wine that Weezer offered and made herself comfortable in the rocking chair in front of the fireplace. The wedding had gone off without any more drama. It had been a beautiful ceremony, filled with love, laughter, and family.

Something that Tamsyn wished she had and understood.

Fred and Anna had given her a roof over her head. They'd provided her with opportunities. They'd opened their home, but they hadn't given her the one thing she desired most. It wasn't completely their fault. In the beginning, she had resisted Anna's affection. All Tamsyn had wanted was her mother. She'd sit by the big picture window, waiting for her mom to appear.

But that never happened.

However, Tamsyn never gave hope. Even to this day, she held on to the idea that her mom was out there,

45

somewhere, and could return any day. It was that concept that drove a wedge between her and Anna. It was an unspoken distance, but it was there.

Tamsyn took a sip of the wine, enjoying the rich flavor. The River family sure knew how to make a good blend. She'd avoided drinking their wine for years, but now there was no reason to boycott. No reason to hold on to a grudge that didn't exist. Carter had done nothing to her or her mother. Nor had Weezer.

Most of the River family had left. The few that remained had shuffled off into the kitchen with Noir and Carter for a card game, leaving her alone with Weezer.

"Are you sure you want to hear this story from me first?" Weezer sat on the sofa, across from Tamsyn.

Weezer was a stunning woman and a contradiction of sorts. Her nails were always perfectly manicured, her graying hair styled to perfection whenever she left the house. Her attire didn't always match. And Weezer had a certain edge to her personality. She didn't care what anyone thought of her and it showed in everything she did.

The people of Candlewood Falls both respected Weezer and feared her wrath. Weezer had a way of getting what she wanted, and she didn't always play fair.

However, she did have a soft side, something Tamsyn had seen firsthand.

"I've asked Anna before, and I've never gotten a

straight answer," Tamsyn admitted. "Anna and Fred took me in. They raised me and I feel like I need to understand this if Noir and I are going to have any chance of making our relationship work. It's going to be hard enough with whispers and potential snide remarks from everyone in this town over what they might believe, even with me presenting the truth about that, which I should have done ten years ago when I found out."

"Sweetheart, the people who matter know the truth." Weezer raised her glass. "Our family, close friends, they never believed it for one second. Carter did that paternity test for you and no one else. If we were worried about it, we would have shouted it from the rooftops."

"So why does Anna dislike you so much?" Tamsyn asked.

Weezer laughed. It wasn't loud or boisterous, but more of a soft, quiet chuckle. "To be totally honest, I can only guess this is what she's holding on to, because Anna and I haven't been close since we were in high school."

"So, you were friends?"

"I wouldn't go that far, but Anna has always wanted to be respected. To be seen as important. More important than anyone else in the room. In high school, she wanted to be class president, but that honor was given to me. She accused me of rigging the election. She demanded a recount."

"That's why she's mad at you?"

"That's only the beginning." Weezer swirled her wine, staring at the liquid hugging the glass. She raised it to her nose and sniffed before taking a sip. "Times were different back then. While college and careers for women were an option and certainly pushed, Anna was the kind of girl who believed the right man would elevate her status in the community more than a career."

"She and Fred were married at twenty-two. They started dating at twenty. He's the love of her life. She has stated she was in love with him for as long as she can remember, but that in high school, Fred was awkward and shy."

"Fred was a little aloof in school," Weezer said. "But Anna wasn't interested in him because his family didn't come from money or have any standing in this community. She had her sights set on Silas."

Tamsyn couldn't help it. She burst out laughing. "I find that hard to believe."

Weezer smiled. "Trust me. Silas was a catch. If I hadn't already been in love with Carter, I would have gone for that man. But Silas wanted nothing to do with Anna, and that drove her crazy. She tried for a year to get him to notice her, to take her out. When that didn't happen, Anna turned her attention to Carter, and that's when our feud began. He was my man and I wasn't going to stand for anyone trying to dig their claws into him."

"I'm struggling to believe that Anna would be interested in Carter at all." Tamsyn had spent a lifetime listening to all the reasons she should stay away from the River family, and Carter being a manipulative man was one of them. "She might dislike you the most, but she has issues with Carter."

"That's because he had to be harsh with her when she wouldn't take no for an answer," Weezer said. "Anna did her best to break us up. She started rumors about me. She would whisper in Carter's ear that I wasn't good enough or that I was flirting with other men, especially after Carter went to college. He didn't go far away, but she once had the audacity to show up at his dorm to give him bogus intel on me and then threw herself at him. That's when he got mean. He tossed her out on her ass and told her that if she ever pulled a stunt like that again, he'd file harassment charges. Sadly, it didn't end there and Carter had to follow through on his threat."

"You've got to be kidding me," Tamsyn said. Anna was a lot of things and a gossip was one of them. The dinner table conversation was always filled with topics of what she'd heard that day about different members of the community. She never cared if the information was true or false; she only cared that she had something juicy to chat about. If it was something negative, she would scowl and say she hoped it wasn't true and act compassionate.

Fred would often tell her to stop gossiping, and Anna's response had always been the same.

That she was just repeating to her family what she'd heard from a reliable source. That it never went further than that.

However, as Tamsyn got older, she found out that Anna enjoyed spreading those rumors to anyone who would listen.

Deep down, Tamsyn knew Anna wasn't a bad person. She craved attention. To be the center of the town. To be the person whom everyone came to.

But again, she wasn't.

That honor went to Weezer and Carter. They were the heartbeat of Candlewood Falls.

"How did Anna handle that?" Tamsyn asked.

"She backed off, but not without a bit of a fight with me." Weezer shifted, taking a slow sip of wine. She leaned forward. "She swore to me that Karma was a bitch and someday, it would come back and bite me in the ass. It was a blanket threat, one that I have ignored. Only, Anna has constantly spoken badly of me every chance she can." Weezer shrugged. "I'm used to it. She's not the only one in this town who has a beef with me. I've made a lot of mistakes in my life, including how I handled things with your mother. I should have never threatened her like that in public—or in front of you. Anything I needed to say to her should have been done in private. That is something I have always regretted. I'm sorry about that."

"I asked Carter this ten years ago, and he didn't have an answer. Maybe you do." Tamsyn rose and strolled across the room, taking a seat next to Weezer on the sofa. "Why do you think my mom lied about having an affair with Carter? Why did she name him as my father so publicly if it wasn't true? Especially after remaining so quiet about it for nearly ten years?"

"We honestly don't know the answer." Weezer patted Tamsyn's leg. "When we confronted your mom, we asked if it was about money and we were willing to give her some. Hell, Carter had been giving her money on and off for a couple of years. That only added fuel to that rumor mill, making Carter look guilty of the crime."

"Carter told me he gave her money after she got arrested and he became her lawyer. He helped her when she was about to lose custody of me."

Weezer nodded. "He didn't want to see that happen. He helped Elizabeth get a job. My husband is a generous man and he hates to see people suffering. Your mom needed help. He tried to get her into ther- apy, and she went at first. Got on the proper medica- tion, but then she'd go off it. Perhaps we were part of the problem, and not the solution, but all we wanted to do was help you and Elizabeth."

"Why?" Tamsyn set her glass on the coffee table and rubbed her temples. "From the outside—and a cop's perspective—the motivation looks suspect."

Weezer laughed. "We all grew up together. While Elizabeth and I weren't close friends, nor was Carter, we had a connection. We hated the way other kids treated her in high school. We always stuck up for her when she got picked on." Weezer lowered her chin. "I know what that feels like. I might have a tough exterior and have the ability to let things roll off my back, but that doesn't mean the things that people say about me don't affect me, especially when I was a teenager. It was damn hard to be part of the crazy family that ran the winery. If you think I'm a whack-a-doodle, my parents were worse. My grandparents were even crazier. Elizabeth's mental illness began showing when she was sixteen. It made others uncomfortable. Carter and I showed her kindness. We always have. After high school, there became a distance with us, but once she had you, we felt a need to help protect you. We told our children to ignore the rumors about your paternity. That they weren't true and to be kind to you."

"I didn't spend much time with your four older kids, but the twins and Zinny were always nice, even if we weren't friends. My mom didn't want me hanging out with them, and Anna made it clear I wasn't allowed to."

"I'm glad my kids were kind, but I'm sorry you were given mixed messages about my family." Weezer took her hand. "That rumor was hard on the twins, especially Noir. Being called a bastard his entire life didn't help that boy. He took it to heart."

"He still does," Tamsyn admitted. "Thank you for

telling me all this. It will be interesting to hear what Anna has to say."

"There is no love lost between me and her, but remember, there are always two sides to every story. Both are based in truth and perception. Just because her side could be different, doesn't mean it's not real to her. It's how she feels about what happened."

Tamsyn jerked her head.

"You didn't expect me to say that about Anna, now did you?"

"No, I didn't," Tamsyn whispered. "I know how Anna can be and she does bend reality to meet her personal desires in life. Sometimes I wonder if she's truly happy."

"My take on that is she settled for Fred."

"That's not fair." Tamsyn might have her own set of issues with Anna, but to attack someone's marriage wasn't cool.

"I'm not saying she doesn't love him now. I have no doubt they are still together for a reason. But back then, he wasn't her type. He wasn't rich. He wasn't overly ambitious. He wasn't the face of the community, like he is now. But when they married, he was a cop and she wanted to make him a politician."

"She still does and Fred wants nothing to do with that. If it wasn't for Carter, I'm not sure he'd be chief of police. Fred is ready to retire. He's waiting for me to be ready to fill his shoes."

Weezer smiled wide. "You'd make for a great chief. You're smart and you've got balls. I admire that."

"Coming from you, that means a lot." Tamsyn had one more thing she wanted to discuss with Weezer. The thought of bringing it up made her pulse race faster than the first time she had to draw her weapon on a perp. While every police officer knew that one day it would happen, it wasn't something they wanted to do. "This thing with me and Noir. It's going to cause a huge ruckus with everyone in town. It will bring up everything we just talked about. I will need to pull out that paternity test at every street corner just to prove I'm not his sibling. While it will be the hardest on me and Noir, I need to know how you and Carter feel about this. I know I'm not everyone's favorite person."

"Oh, sweetheart." Weezer squeezed her hands, hard. "I'm sorry if we made you feel that way, but to be fair, you haven't made it easy for us to be friendly. And we've kept a safe distance out of our respect for you and Elizabeth. But make no mistake. We have no ill will toward you. If you make our son happy, we will support the two of you. This family has weathered far worse than this little scandal. It will pass."

"I hope you're right." Tamsyn sucked in a shallow breath.

"You must care deeply for my boy; otherwise, you wouldn't subject yourself to the ridicule that is coming."

Tamsyn reached for her wine and tipped it back like

a shot of whiskey. It was one thing to admit her feelings to herself and to Noir. But to express it to his mother—his family—and to the world, was something entirely different. "I tried not to. And it's not like it came out of left field. Noir and I have been chatting for years. We've danced around this for a long time, pushing our feelings aside and trying to be friends. But we couldn't fight it anymore."

"You can't fight true love."

Tamsyn coughed. Love was too strong of a word.

Thankfully, Noir strolled into the family room. "You two look chummy."

"We had a nice chat." Weezer stood. "Time to go find my new daughter-in-law and give her a piece of my mind." She kissed Noir's cheek. "Tamsyn's a keeper. Don't fuck it up."

Noir chuckled. "Yes, Mother."

Heat rose to Tamsyn's cheek. This was not the reception she had expected. Her heart swelled. Now, if only she could get Anna and Fred on board.

"Hey, babe." Noir lifted her off the sofa and took her in his arms. "Told you my family liked you."

"One hurdle overcome, but we have a million more." She wrapped her arms around his strong shoulders.

"Would you mind driving me back to Nebbiolo's place? I want to grab as much stuff as I can tonight and bring it back to the cottage so the newlyweds can have the place to themselves. When you get off work in the morning, you can swing by before I have to go to work."

She groaned. "I don't think I'll enjoy the fact your parents will be able to see me coming and going."

"They won't bother you. They might be over the top and have been known to meddle, but they have always respected their children's privacy." His lips landed on her mouth in a soft, but potent kiss. It was tender, loving, and sweet.

"All right, but we better get going. I need to be at work in an hour and Fred runs a tight ship." She had plenty of time; that wasn't the problem. She feared Anna had already informed Fred of her *relationship status*. Fred might not have the same problems with the River family. He respected Carter. If it weren't for him, Fred wouldn't have his current position as chief of police, a position he hadn't necessarily wanted ten years ago. But Carter thought he'd make a better one than old man Harper.

That was certainly true and Tamsyn was glad Fred took the job.

Fred didn't take issue with any of the River kids. At least not as adults. But he did have problems with Weezer. Mostly because he always took Anna's side anytime Anna ranted about Weezer.

This was going to be one hell of a night.

4

NOIR

"I appreciate the help." Noir cracked open two bottles of ice-cold beer and handed one to Merlot. "I couldn't stand to be around Nebbiolo and June a second longer."

"They are a bit disgusting." Merlot laughed. He plopped himself down on the sofa in the small cottage, resting his feet on the coffee table in front of the bed. "But she seems nice and brings out the best in your twin."

"I feel like I lost an appendage."

"That's not a bad thing. You two always had an odd attachment toward each other. More so than the rest of us."

Noir pulled out a bag of chips and dip his mother had sent him. She'd also stocked the fridge and cabinets with a ton of food, claiming she'd overbought for the wedding. But Noir knew she'd most likely taken all the tasty treats from her pantry and filled his because that's what she did. He knew better than to argue. He set them on the table and eased onto the couch. "That twin bond is different than a sibling bond."

"I wouldn't know." Merlot tapped his beer against Noir's. "You're the last single River. Well, the last one who's not married. How serious are you and Tamsyn? Is it love? Heavy like? Are we talking about moving in together?"

"You're worse than Mom." Noir took a hearty sip. He'd been fielding questions all day, even from Corbin, who wanted to be kept informed via messenger while he was training with the Army. Noir couldn't believe he had a nephew who was twenty-one years old. It baffled his brain. Even though he hadn't known Corbin until a few months ago, he fit into the family as though he'd always been there.

"Inquiring minds want to know." Merlot arched a brow. "I can't say she's your type because I've only seen you take out a few ladies; none were actual girlfriends."

Noir could count his girlfriends on one hand. He never really dated until college. The first real relationship had lasted his sophomore and junior years, but the only person who knew about Tina had been Nebbiolo. Tina started off as a nice girl. They had fun together and had a lot in common. But soon, as it often did, things got weird. She resented the closeness he shared with his twin and gave him an ultimatum.

He chose his brother.

His second major relationship had been a woman he worked with.

Same problem.

Since then, he dated here and there, but nothing worth noting.

And now there was Tamsyn.

"That's a complicated question to answer," Noir said.

"Why?"

"Tamsyn has been adamant for the last month that we keep things on the down-low. Because of that, I haven't let myself get too attached. However, I care for her, a lot. Perhaps more than I have anyone I've ever been with, but we've barely put it out there. I'm not sure she's ready to go screaming anything from the rooftops and I don't want to pressure her."

"Let me give you a piece of unsolicited older brotherly advice." Merlot cocked a brow and lowered his chin. "Don't wait to express yourself. It's not manly and only serves to cause problems in the long run. If she doesn't know how you feel, don't leave her to guess."

Noir chuckled. "Oh, I think it's easier for me in that department, believe it or not, than her."

Lights flashed across the window. He glanced at his watch. "It's eleven thirty. I wonder if Tamsyn forgot something." Leaping off the sofa, he raced toward the door.

"I better get going home and help my wife finishing

packing for our honeymoon." Merlot stood and rinsed his beer out in the sink. "This is technically my wedding night."

Noir pulled back the door and blinked. "Anna? What are you doing here?" His heart dropped like a brick to his toes. "Oh no. Is Tamsyn okay? Was she hurt?"

"No. No. Nothing like that." Anna clutched her purse as if Noir was going to rip it from her shoulder. "I'd like to speak with you." She peered over his shoulder. "In private."

"I was just leaving." Merlot scooted past them both. "Take care, little brother." He nodded. "Good to see you, Anna. Be sure to say hello to Fred." He disappeared out the door and down the path fast as lighting.

Wonderful.

Anna said nothing and without asking, she forced her way into Noir's home. "This place is interesting."

"How did you know I was here and not at the house I shared with my twin?" Noir asked.

"I'm married to the chief of police." She set her bag on the table, pulled back a chair, and sat down. "There isn't much in this town that doesn't get by me."

"By all means, make yourself at home." Noir contemplated whether he wanted to sit or stand. He opted not to be rude and eased into a seat across from Anna. "What brings you by this late at night?"

"I'm incredibly concerned about my daughter."

Noir cleared his throat. He knew how much Tamsyn

hated it when Anna flippantly tossed that word around. As a kid, she often referred to Anna as her guardian, which would send Anna into a tailspin, especially at mother-daughter functions. Tamsyn hated those and resented Anna for wanting to attend.

But this moment wasn't the time for him to correct Anna, even though Tamsyn would have.

"Why?" he asked.

"For starters, I don't think it's a good idea for you to be dating Tamsyn." Anna dug into her purse and pulled out her cell. "I don't have to be told what a wonderful man your father is, even though he's done some shady things." She held up her hand. "He's certainly proved his worth in this community, and Lord knows he has to be a saint for putting up with Weezer."

"Those are my parents. I mean no disrespect to you, ma'am, but I'm not going to sit here and listen to you speak unkindly about either of them."

"Well, you're going to have to hear a lot of unkind things if you continue this ungodly relationship with Tamsyn, young man. I understand that there is no basis to the rumor about Carter and Elizabeth. But this town has a long memory, and Weezer was not kind to Tamsyn's mother. On any occasion, even if she says she was. You were just a little boy. You don't remember all that transpired. Elizabeth was my friend. She confided in me and that argument your mother had with Elizabeth wasn't the only time Weezer made sweeping threats."

"I need to stop you right there." Noir rubbed the back of his neck. "None of this has anything to do with me and Tamsyn. I appreciate your concern, but we're adults. Capable of making our own decisions. We can handle whatever the people of this town decide to toss at us, and I doubt it will be what you think." Noir wanted to add that Anna was full of shit. That she'd never been a real friend to Elizabeth. That the only time she'd ever done anything nice for Tamsyn's mother had been when it would make Anna look good. Otherwise, she stayed clear of Elizabeth, calling her the town loon. She once even stated that Elizabeth was crazier than Weezer.

Noir had been present in the local coffee shop for that one.

But he refrained. Besides being too tired, pissing Anna off to the point he had no chance of ever having any decent relationship with Anna and Fred wasn't a good idea.

He cared for Tamsyn too much to do that.

"It's going to be hell, and Tamsyn is the one who is going to get hurt. If you care for her at all, you'll end this right now."

"I'm sorry, Anna. But I'm not going to do that." He stood. "You've said your piece. It's late. Please drive home safely."

"I'm not done yet." She tapped her cell. "I need you to speak to your mom about something for me."

This should be rich. "About what?"

"The Holiday Showcase." She held up her phone. "She's completely taken over, without holding it to a vote with the committee. That's unfair and unreasonable. I tried talking to Weezer, but she's not willing to budge. Everyone on the committee is afraid to challenge her, with the exception of me and Mrs. Cummings. Please explain to your mother that there are other venues in town and other people willing to step up and do the showcase. It needs to be voted on, proper."

"I'm not getting involved in that." Noir couldn't believe that Anna would even ask him to do such a thing. It was utterly absurd.

"Yes, you are. Or you will leave me no choice but to show the committee this note that I've been sitting on for twenty years." She rose, shoving her phone in his face.

He took it, glancing at the scanned in, handwritten note.

Anna,

I'm scared. It's getting worse. The threats are constant. I don't know what to do. I'm afraid if I don't do what she says, she'll follow through.

Elizabeth.

"Have you shown this to Tamsyn? To Fred? To anyone?" Noir asked, handing the cell back.

"Tamsyn has not seen it, but Fred has, and I told the police when Elizabeth disappeared all about Weezer and her unrelenting harassment."

"That note says nothing about my mother," Noir said. "Threatening to show it to the committee if I don't try to stop my mom from having the Holiday Showcase at the winery is falling on deaf ears." He turned and opened the door. "I'm sorry. I won't do it. I hope we can put our differences aside because I care about Tamsyn and I'm not going anywhere."

Anna scoffed. "We'll see about that." She snatched her purse, tugging it over her shoulder. "May I use your bathroom before I leave?"

"Sure." He pointed over her shoulder.

"Thank you." She turned on her heel.

He waited for the next ten minutes as patiently as he could. He had thought about telling her no, but that would have been rude and his mother had raised him better. Well, mostly better than that.

Anna stepped from the bathroom. "Please think about what I said. I don't want to have to bring up that note in front of everyone, but I will. Make no mistake." She scurried past him and out the door.

"Well, that was fun." Noir let out a long breath. He pulled out his phone and shot off a text to Tamsyn. He didn't like telling her about Anna's visit that way, but she was only a few minutes from clocking in, and she most likely wouldn't have answered the call. If and when she had time during her patrol, she'd call, and he'd pick up.

He tapped star one and plopped back onto the bed.

His father picked up on the second ring. "It's late. Is something wrong with your new accommodations?"

"No. I love the cottage. Thank you," he said. "I don't know if you noticed or not, but I had an odd visitor."

"Your mother and I are in bed, so we didn't. I take it whoever showed up wasn't necessarily a welcomed guest."

"It was Anna."

"Jesus. What the hell did she want?" his father asked in a tone that indicated more concern than frustration of being disturbed at a late hour.

"A plethora of things, but the one that kicked me in the gut was she has a note from Elizabeth that she's never shown Tamsyn. It was cryptic, but it implies someone was threatening her."

"Let me guess. Anna believes that person was your mother."

"Exactly, only the note doesn't say that. It was handwritten and scanned into her phone. She said Fred's seen it and that she's spoken to the cops about all the times Mom threatened Elizabeth. She even claimed that she and Elizabeth were friends."

His dad laughed, but it wasn't a funny haha laugh. It was sarcastic in tone and nature. "Anna did her best to point the finger at your mom when Elizabeth first disappeared. She ranted to anyone who would listen that Weezer must have done something. When Tamsyn accused Weezer, Anna played right into that, but no note was ever brought up. Not by her or by Fred."

"Well, it might show up tonight or tomorrow."

"That should be interesting. Thanks for letting me know," his dad said. "You doing okay?"

"I knew things would be weird. I worried about what you and Mom would say. Or my siblings. But I knew I would have your support. I figured we'd get backlash from some people, including Anna, but I honestly didn't expect something like this."

"That damn Holiday Showcase makes everyone in this town nuts, including your mother... ouch. That hurt, Weezer."

Noir laughed. Growing up, he never comprehended his parents' relationship. That lack of understanding had caused him uncertainty and a lot of grief. In the past few years, he'd grown to adore his parents' romance, their love for one another, and their dedication to their family. He didn't agree with everything they'd done, but their hearts had been in the right place. "I'll see you tomorrow."

"Good night, son. Sleep well."

Noir stared at his phone.

No text back from Tamsyn.

He shouldn't be surprised. Not that Candlewood Falls was a crime ridden community, but Tamsyn took her position as a police officer seriously and she might not want to deal with a personal issue such as this until off duty hours.

Tamsyn

Tamsyn stared at the text from Noir. "Shit," she mumbled. Fucking Anna and her crazy antics. When Tamsyn had been twelve, Anna had talked her into performing in the Holiday Showcase. Only, their talent had been all focused on Anna and her singing, which was horrible.

Tamsyn was to play the piano, something she enjoyed in the privacy of her own home. She still enjoyed it, and she liked to sing, but she wasn't overly talented in either category. However, to appease her guardian, she agreed.

Only, Anna had thrown a hissy fit about everything that Weezer was doing and the committee collectively voted to toss Anna out of the show. It didn't happen often, but they did have a limited number of spots. Anna fumed over it for months. She vowed to get Weezer back and she never let her forget her poor choice in pushing Tamsyn out of the showcase.

That wasn't what happened, since Weezer had told everyone that Tamsyn was free to perform, just not with Anna.

Tamsyn squared her shoulders, looped her fingers into her uniform belt, and strolled into Fred's office. "You wanted to see me?"

"Close the door and take a seat." Fred waved his hand toward the chair in front of his desk, not bothering to stand. For man in his early sixties, he was still quite attractive. He stood six feet tall, with a muscular frame. His hair had thinned and grayed some. He had deep lines around his eyes, showing the stress of his job. His eyes were dark brown and soulful. He carried the weight of the town on his shoulders, and it was a responsibility he didn't take lightly. "I stayed late because this couldn't wait until tomorrow night's dinner."

"So, this is a personal chat, not a professional one." Tamsyn respected Fred both as her superior and as the man who took her in when she had no one. He didn't have to do that, and she would be forever grateful to both him and Anna.

However, there were times when she wished Fred would stand up to Anna. Her childhood had been filled with ridicule and shame. While her home life had been a safe haven, she had always felt like an outsider, especially when it came to Anna. As if she'd been an interloper in her life. It didn't matter that Anna met every physical need she had because she lacked the one quality she needed most.

The love of a true family.

Fred tried to pull it all together, but he failed too.

It wasn't entirely their fault. In the beginning, they gave her space. Time to get used to their living arrangement and respecting her dream that her mom would soon return. But over time, Anna wanted the town to see them as a happy family from the outside, when they were merely three people who lived under one roof.

"It's a little bit of both." He leaned back, folding his arms. "Anna is quite upset and to be honest, I'm not thrilled about this situation with the River family either."

"If you're referring to me dating Noir, it's not a situation." She gripped the sides of the chair. "I didn't mean for you and Anna to find out this way. I had intended on telling you tonight. Anna barging into the Rivers' home was an unexpected complication."

"That's an interesting way of putting it," Fred said. "How long have you and Noir been secretly an item?"

"A little over a month." She resented how this felt as though she were being interrogated. She wasn't a child who stayed out past curfew. Not that she'd ever done that. She'd been a model teenager regarding grades and following Fred's rules. She did, however, occasionally break Anna's.

"Why didn't you tell us?"

"Partly because I knew how Anna would react, and partly because I wanted to keep it private until I was ready to deal with the bullshit this town is going to throw at us." She shifted, lifting an envelope from her back pocket that had been burning a hole in it for the last ten minutes. She pushed it across the table. "I'm starting to think I should take out an ad in the paper or maybe release this to the press."

Fred lifted it, raising it to the light. "What is this?"

"A paternity test I had Carter take ten years ago, proving he's not my father."

"Well, I knew that wasn't true." Fred whistled. "Why on God's green earth have you been sitting on this for all these years?" He glanced over the document. "We've talked about this. I've chatted with Carter. But why didn't you give me this? I'm shocked that Weezer hasn't been shouting it from a bullhorn."

"I have a dozen reasons why, but they all seem stupid now," she said. "I care about Noir. I want you to be okay with this. I need you to be on my side."

"You mean when it comes to Anna? Or with everyone else?"

"Both," Tamsyn said.

"When it comes to Anna, that's a tough one." Fred handed the paper back and rested his arms on the desk. "Weezer has never made it easy for Anna in this town. Not when they were kids and certainly not now. I don't see Anna accepting this relationship. I know you don't see us as your parents. I understand that, but Anna doesn't. And she only wants what's best for you, and she won't see Noir as being anything other than bad."

"He's a good man, and you know it."

Fred cocked his head. "I never said he wasn't. But he's a River. He's Weezer's son. Anna will never change

her mind regarding how she feels about that family."
Fred ran a hand over his mouth, his index finger and
thumb meeting at the tip of his square jaw. "I'm not a
fan of Weezer either, but I have no beef with Noir or
the rest of her kids. That said, there are hundreds of
other men in this town. You had to pick him? Really?
That's an uphill battle that I can't imagine will end
well."

"Once the gossip settles down, and it will, time will
tell."

"Look, I love you like my own, you know that."

While she believed Fred cared deeply, she had never
felt that strong bond she should have for the two
people who gave her so many opportunities. She
carried a pang of guilt for that.

"The moment anyone in this town gets wind of you
dating Noir, and that will be by morning light, I'm sure,
you will be dealing with the same whispers, same
stares, same bullshit that turned you into the most
quiet, reserved little girl I brought into my home at the
age of ten. You didn't blossom into the strong-willed,
stubborn pain in the ass woman you are today until you
turned twenty and grew a voice."

"I do have you to thank for that, but Anna wouldn't
mind squelching my tenacity, and she hates half my
opinions."

"She doesn't like to be challenged," Fred said.

"No, she doesn't." Tamsyn rolled her neck. "I know
I've asked this a dozen times. But I'm going to ask it

again. Do you have any idea who my biological father is?"

"I wish I did because I'd like to give that man a piece of my mind," Fred said. "Anna and I could never have children. It's something that I wish I could have given her, but it wasn't in the cards. We were looking into adoption when you came into our lives. Something we're grateful for, but not the circumstances in which it happened. However, if I do ever come face-to-face with the man who got your mom pregnant and walked away, I will toss my badge temporarily in the garbage and kick the shit out of him."

Tamsyn had heard the speech a million times and each time it warmed her heart. Fred wasn't a fiery man. He didn't get passionate about many things. He was a rule guy and following the letter of the law mattered; it was the one thing he truly believed in. Seeing that kind of emotion emoting from his eyes was the one time she truly felt loved by him, and she would always hold on to that.

"You should know I did do the whole DNA thing. Finding my father is important to me."

Fred nodded. "I wish you hadn't simply because you know how I feel about having your DNA in the system, but I understand."

Tamsyn stood. "May I be excused? I have streets to patrol."

"I expect to see you for dinner tomorrow tonight and we'll work through this."

"I'll be there." She turned on her heel and double-timed it out the door.

"What the hell did he want?" Eddy Jenson, her partner, asked. He leaned against the wall not far from what they referred to as the bullpen, an open room where all the local cops shared desk space.

She might as well let the cat out of the bag herself. "I got a lecture about my new boyfriend." She made her way to her desk and snagged the keys to the patrol vehicle. "Fred does not approve and Anna is fit to be tied."

"Sweet Jesus. Who the hell are you dating? Someone in lockup?"

"Worse. Noir River."

Eddy stopped dead in his tracks. "Wait one second. I'm sorry to be a dick, but I heard about a rumor back in the day—"

"Carter is not my father. Noir is not my half brother. I have the proof if you need to see it."

Eddy laughed. "Oh, no. I believe you, but it's all anyone is going to be able to think about."

"I'm painfully aware." She pushed open the back door, heading to the parking lot. "But you could help me by telling everyone who brings it up that it's not true."

"I've got your six," Eddy said. "I knew Noir in high school. I mean, as anyone could know him. He pretty much only hung out with his twin. But I've had a few beers with him this past year. He seems like a cool guy."

"Just misunderstood." She yanked open the driver's side door.

"Isn't everyone in that family. I mean, come on. They have Weezer for a mother."

"She's actually a really nice woman, once you get to know her."

Eddy slipped into the passenger seat. During the day shifts, they didn't always go out in tandem, but at night, with the rash of crimes that had been happening in the next town over, Fred had decided he wanted two-man teams on the streets. That meant double shifts and overtime.

Tamsyn didn't mind the hours or the extra cash. But there were some officers who had families and were already overworked.

Eddy wasn't one of them.

"I've had my share of run-ins with the Weezer." Eddy laughed as he buckled in. "I've always found if you're not afraid and treat her with respect, she's a pretty normal person, but I'd never want to be on her bad side."

No truer words had ever been spoken.

"Let's hope for a quiet night."

5

CARTER

Carter stood at the window in the master bedroom. He stared at the rising sun as it peeked over the horizon, shedding light on the vineyard. He'd spent a lifetime protecting his wife. His family. He'd made hard choices that most people didn't understand.

He'd changed his last name, taking his wife's, so that his children would have the same name as their legacy. He'd taken hell for that one. People in the town believed his wife controlled his every move.

Not.

Although, everything he did was in part to save Weezer from herself. That woman could be the most stubborn human known to man.

But he loved her with every fiber of his being and would move heaven and earth to make sure she was happy and safe.

"Here you go, my love." Weezer appeared in the bedroom with two mugs of coffee, handing him one. "Just the way you like it."

"Thanks, dear." He kissed her sweet lips. "You tossed and turned all night."

"So did you." She leaned against the windowsill. "Can I safely assume your thoughts were with Tamsyn, Noir, and that damned stupid note?"

"Among other things," he said. "I understand why you didn't tell her everything, but did we make the right decision in keeping that from her?"

"We reported it," Weezer said. "It should be in the missing persons file. She should know."

"She's never once asked me about it and she and I have had some long conversations over the years. Not a day has gone by where I haven't wondered what happened to Elizabeth. If she's dead or alive. If she's dead, was she killed? Did she take her own life? And if so, was it because of what we said or did?"

Weezer rested her hand on his shoulder. "We never did anything but try to help Elizabeth, and you know it. Elizabeth was in the wrong, and we were defending your honor and protecting our children. Let's not forget we were trying to protect Tamsyn as well."

Deep down, Carter knew that was true, but it didn't change that hindsight was perfect vision, and he could see twenty years later that he could have done things differently. "I'm hoping Noir can get his hands on a copy of that letter. I'd like to see it."

"Since Noir isn't going to try to talk me into asking the committee to have a vote, she might hold true to her threat to show the committee this afternoon." Weezer waggled her finger. "Which burns my ass because everyone on that committee wants me to step up. No one, except Mrs. Cummings, wants to take on the showcase this late in the game."

Carter arched a brow. "Honey. While that may be true, you do tend to take over."

"Someone has to do it, and I'm not going to change because Anna wants the spotlight and believes I'm doing this because I want to drum up business for the winery or because she thinks I'm an attention whore."

"The latter is a little bit true." He made the inch sign.

"Carter River." She hip checked him. "I should cut you off from pleasure for a week for that statement."

He kissed her cheek. "I know your heart is in the right place and you're doing this more to help Silas, Claudia, and the community. Just own that you enjoy coming to the rescue."

Her lips curled into a smile. "I do put on a good show."

"That you do, darling," he said, letting out a long breath. "I wish I knew who Tamsyn's father was. That's all she wants to know, but that's like finding a needle in a haystack and my list of suspects is few and far between."

"I didn't mention to Tamsyn that Elizabeth sold her

body for money and drugs. She's a smart young girl and a cop. I would think she knows."

"She never came out and said it, but she saw men coming in and out of the house. We discussed it because she wondered if any of them could have been her father." Carter blew into his mug as he watched Tamsyn's police vehicle roll past the house toward the cottage. "She didn't recognize any of the men. They weren't locals, except for three. Me, Fred, and Sheriff Morton. We know why I was there, and Fred and Morton were only there to arrest Elizabeth or warn her for something."

"Morton is in prison. We know what kind of man he turned out to be. And Fred always went too easy on Elizabeth," Weezer said.

"It was a difficult situation and jail wasn't where she belonged." Carter set his mug on the dresser. He looped his arm around his wife. "She needed more than any of us could give her. I tried. I really did. The year before she disappeared, she was doing so well. She was back on her meds, going to therapy. I don't understand what happened."

Weezer put her mug next to his and cupped his face. "You always believed she was in her right mind when she came after us. That she hadn't been drinking or doing drugs. But why would she blatantly lie about you being Tamsyn's father after all that we did if she was stable? It makes no sense."

"It's weighed heavily on my mind all these years.

Our son has been in love with that girl since middle school. We knew it was only a matter of time before this happened. I'm contemplating giving that girl what little I have from the private investigator I hired to find Elizabeth."

"The only thing Gino has uncovered is that Elizabeth never boarded any train."

"The cops have a ticket purchased in her name," Carter said. "But Gino—nor the cops—could never find a witness to her getting on that train or any evidence she landed in Florida. She never used her credit card again. The one clue we had turned out to be a dead end. But what concerns me is that her bank account was depleted hours before your fight. And what we still haven't told Tamsyn is that Elizabeth texted you an hour before that altercation, asking you to meet."

"I should have never gone," Weezer said.

"Why didn't you tell Tamsyn about that text?"

"The conversation was mostly about Anna's problems with us. It only circled to Elizabeth near the end and that text is just one more thing that shows how unstable Elizabeth was, especially because it didn't make sense," Weezer said. "She wanted to talk. To clear the air. She made it sound like she wanted to apologize; instead, when she saw me, she went right into how I needed to get you to do the right thing."

"But even you said Elizabeth didn't seem like she was on drugs. That she seemed angry and nervous. But we both know how she was when she was not on her meds and using. I'll agree that she was acting strangely, but it wasn't because she was out of her mind. Something happened a couple of weeks before your public fight with her. Something that made her accuse me. That's what I need Gino to focus on. That's where we'll find the answers to her disappearance."

"I've always wondered who took that video of us fighting and anonymously sent it to the press."

"That could have been anyone."

"Including Anna," Weezer said.

"I've thought about that. But she's never gone after you anonymously. She's always been up front and in your face. If it was her, she'd want you to know."

Weezer nodded. "She does like the attention more than I do."

Carter laughed. "I wouldn't go that far."

Noir

Noir had never once thought about living in the cottage or anywhere near the winery in all his thirty years. He'd kept his family at a safe distance, and for what? As he stood on the front stoop, watching Tamsyn's patrol car ease down the long, windy dirt road, he couldn't think of a good reason.

While his parents' divorce never made sense to him,

it did to them. They had always been there for him, showing him love and kindness. They encouraged him in school. To find those things that made his heart sing, but he never had the will or the courage to step away from his twin and live his life.

Until now.

Tamsyn had made everything possible. She was everything he wanted to be.

Strong. Confident. And didn't give a fuck about what anyone thought—except for one thing. She cared about her mother, leaving a dark mark on her psyche a mile long.

In many ways, Tamsyn was like his mother. Everyone in Candlewood Falls madly misunderstood them both. They both carried the burden of someone else's decisions—and mistakes. And they both loved as passionately as they judged.

Her vehicle rolled to a stop and she stepped from behind the wheel. "What are you doing out here? It's freezing."

"I saw you coming, so I thought I'd greet you properly."

"If you wanted to do that, you'd be naked in bed because I'm oddly turned on by the fact I might get laid on The River Winery." She reached into the back of her patrol vehicle and snagged her overnight bag.

He burst out laughing. "There's no might about it. I'd say you're at a hundred percent." He pressed his hand on the small of her back, guiding her into the cottage. "I brought over half my stuff last night, thanks to Merlot."

"That was nice of him to help on his wedding night. I take it he's the one who drove my car over." She stepped through the door.

"He did." Noir nodded. "I enjoyed hanging out one-on-one with him."

"I'm so happy to see you getting along so well with your family."

"It was a long time coming."

She shimmied out of her parka and handed it to him before she undid her gun belt and held it up. "I need a secure place to put this."

"Since I know how you need that thing close, I made sure the right nightstand was empty, just for you."

"Aww, now that's a good boyfriend."

He took her into his arms, heaving her to his chest. "I like the sound of that."

She rolled her eyes. "When I got back from patrol, everyone in the office knew. How does shit like this spread like wildfire in this town? We only told your family."

"Who hired a local photographer." He pressed his finger over her lips. "Just because my dad paid him an extra couple of hundred to keep his fat trap shut, doesn't mean he did and I don't mean to be a dick, but I wouldn't put it past Anna to stir the pot by already either giving that note to the Holiday Showcase committee or dropping little juicy bombs about us where she can."

"Anna's a lot of things, but she won't want to deal with what she perceives as a scandal. She'll keep it to herself if she thinks it will make her look bad."

"Except we're outing ourselves." Noir untucked her shirt, running his hands up her back, enjoying the way she arched into his body. Her skin felt like the finest silk, not that he'd ever had that between his fingers, but he could imagine it would be similar to Tamsyn.

"I don't want to talk about this anymore. All I want to do is get naked with you, sleep for a few hours, and then go face the music with Fred and Anna." She patted Noir's chest. "I was hoping you'd come with me tonight."

He cocked his head. "Are you serious? After she showed up here, warning me off? I don't think that's a good idea."

"You're just chicken." She inched back, unbuttoning her shirt and tossing it to the side. Quickly, she shed her uniform slacks, and he raced to the bed. Carefully, she unloaded her weapon, doing what she needed to do for safety, before placing it in the drawer. She pulled back the sheets and jumped in.

He ripped off his sweatshirt and running pants. "It's not that. I have no problem speaking my mind with Anna. Nor Fred. And that's the real issue. I might not be able to bite my tongue. I don't want to cause problems for you or us."

"And if I want you there as much as you wanted me to go to your brother's wedding?" She straddled him, releasing her bra, covering her breasts with her hands.

This was the first time he'd had a strong emotional connection to a woman. The few ladies he'd been in a long-term relationship with never consumed his thoughts the way Tamsyn had. Perhaps his family was right about Tamsyn. Even when they avoided each other in public after she accused his mother of possibly harming his, they still chatted in text. Sometimes it had been heated because he'd been pissed. But in the end, he understood all Tamsyn wanted were answers she thought his family had.

"Then I'll go." Gently, he traced a finger from her belly button, up to the center of her chest, batting her hands away.

Tamsyn had to be the most beautiful woman he'd ever met and not just on the outside. She had a tough exterior. She had to, considering the way some people treated her in this town. He understood that. It was one of the things that had bonded them together as children.

They had hidden their friendship because they had to, much like they had hidden their relationship.

She'd learned to have a thick skin and to take things on the chin. She did her best not to let the good citizens of Candlewood Falls rattle her confidence, though occasionally, he saw it slip.

But on the inside, Tamsyn was sweet. Kind. Genuine. And honest. What you saw was what you got.

She leaned forward, kissing his lips tenderly. "Thank you."

"We're in this together." He cupped the back of her neck, drawing her close, needing to feel her skin against his. Knowing they were out in the open made being with her different. It made it real. The fire growing in his heart exploded like a bomb. The intense heat raced through his system, igniting every cell.

He flipped her to her back, kissing his way across her neck, licking her sweet skin, tasting every inch he could. He sucked on one nipple, then the other, in a desperate need to fill her every desire.

A loud hunger filled his soul.

Tugging at her panties, he pulled them to her ankles. She protected the streets, making sure everyone in Candlewood Falls was safe.

He wanted to be the person who took care of her, tending to her needs, wants, and being the man she turned to when she needed a strong shoulder.

"Oh my God." She threaded her fingers through his hair, clutching tightly. "You're too good at this." Her soft moans echoed in his ears, encouraging him to bring her over the edge.

But he wanted to savor her a little while longer. To tease her. To bring her there slowly.

"Yes. Please, Noir." She raised her hips, rolling them against his mouth. "I need this."

He caved to her wishes. In that moment, he knew he'd do anything she wanted. He'd been lost, and she guided him home. She showed him a pathway to a life with his family, and she stood by his side the whole time, even when she shouldn't have.

She tensed, grabbing the sheets, balling them in her hands. She jerked, shaking her head, moaning, "Yes, yes."

Her climax filled his mouth. But he didn't relent. He continued lapping, teasing her, bringing on a second one that was just as powerful as the first.

"You've got to stop." She pulled his hair.

He chuckled. "You didn't want to go for a third?" He pressed his lips firmly on her stomach.

She gasped for air. "I think I'm good, but now it's your turn." She smiled wickedly, giving him a good shove, rolling him to his back. Wasting no time, she curled her fingers around his length, stroking gently, gradually increasing the pressure.

Tugging at her hair tie, he released her long, dark hair. He ran his fingers through the strands, pooling it on the top of her head.

He hissed when she licked her lips and brought her mouth to the tip, taking him in slowly. He could barely fill his lungs with oxygen as he watched her give him the most exquisite pleasure. This wasn't just sex. It was so much more. A quiet fear lodged in his throat. He couldn't honestly say he'd ever been in love before. He'd cared for his past girlfriend, but never enough to want to spend every waking—and sleeping—moment with them.

"Come here," he whispered.

She climbed on top, easing him into her warm body.

Gripping her hips, he steadied her, holding her intense gaze. He stared into her beautiful, loving eyes, searching for the same emotions that had filled his heart with the power of a rocket punching through the atmosphere.

Her chest rose and fell with every short, choppy breath she took. Her lips parted, and she gasped at the unspoken words that needed to be expressed.

Reaching up, he fanned his thumb across her cheek. "Are you as scared as I am?"

"Terrified."

Having her on top would normally be his preferred position. However, this moment called for a change of pace. Carefully, he rolled, cradling her head in his palms. He kissed her nose. "I've been in love with you for a long time; I just wasn't able to admit it to myself, much less you." There. He'd said it. Out loud, to the woman he never wanted to live without.

She blinked out a tear.

His breath stuck in his lungs. "Shit. The last thing I wanted to do was upset you."

"You haven't. I'm not sure where that came from. I'm not normally the emotional type."

"That I know." He kissed her wet cheek. "Maybe this wasn't the right time to—"

"No." She wrapped her legs tight around his waist. "It was perfect and I love you too, Noir. I really do."

He kissed her, hard. It was filled with passion, love, and a promise to always be there, no matter what. This was the woman he was meant to be with. To share his life with. Their hearts and souls belonged to each other.

The shock of it all rumbled through his system like a high-speed train approaching. It was faint at first, building slowly, until it was right there, racing past.

He held her for a long moment afterward, running his fingers gently over her spine. Shifting to his side, he pulled the covers over their bodies, gazing into her soulful eyes. He smiled.

"That was epic in a few different ways."

"Those weren't shallow words." He brushed the hair from her face.

"I know. I meant them too."

"I wish I didn't have to leave you and go to work." He ran his thumb over her lower lip. "I'd like nothing better than to curl up and spend the day in this bed with you."

"I need a few hours of sleep," she said. "But do I need to worry about your family barging in on me? Your mom has been great, but she has a reputation for not respecting people's personal space."

"Don't believe everything you hear about my mom. The majority of it comes from people who have either wronged her or this family. Or it's idle gossip regarding things people don't understand." He tossed his legs to the side of the bed and hiked up his boxers. "If your car is here, they won't come in unannounced. They know you had the night shift, and I can remind them to leave you alone."

"Thanks, I appreciate it."

He leaned over and kissed her tenderly. "I love you."

A smile spread across her face. "I like how that sounds."

"So do I." With a newfound spring in his step, he strolled toward the bathroom.

"Hey, Noir."

"Yeah?" He glanced over his shoulder.

She sat up, letting the covers pool to her waist, exposing her perfect breasts. "Think of me and how I love you back while you're at work."

He groaned. "I'm going to need a cold shower."

6

NOIR

Noir sat in the back office at the winery, staring at a pile of paperwork. God, he hated this part of his job. He'd rather be out on the road, selling products, not going through spreadsheets, doing both Nebbiolo's and Merlot's jobs. He understood that he and his twin were at the same level—and position—in the family business. However, since they had come on full-time, Noir had been required to spend more time doing administrative work than Nebbiolo at the request of his siblings.

That he didn't comprehend.

"Hey, big brother." Zinny came bouncing through the door, sipping on her favorite fruity drink. She handed him a cup of the same from Green Bean, the local coffee shop. "I thought you might like one."

He laughed. His little sister constantly tried to get the rest of the family hooked on her strawberry treat.

He took it, sipped, and smiled. He had to admit, he'd grown to enjoy it like a nice liquid dessert in the afternoon. "Thanks."

"I can't believe Mom gave Nebbiolo an entire week off after the stunt he pulled," Zinny said. "I don't care that June is as nice as they come and he's turned into a chatty Cathy, sharing things about himself that only you and I knew because he doesn't talk to anyone else, he was a dick to leave you holding the bag."

"Water under the bridge." Noir leaned back, taking another big slurp. "I'm just glad the unnatural umbilical cord between the two of us has finally been severed."

"That's one way to look at it," Zinny said. "But still, it leaves you doing triple duty."

"About that." He tapped his fingers on the pile of papers. "I've been meaning to ask why he gets more time selling, and I'm stuck in here, but have been too afraid to broach the subject with Merlot and Mom."

"I can answer that." Zinny climbed up on the desk, swinging her legs back and forth. She had more energy than anyone in the family. It could be because she was the youngest, but Zinny had their mom's personality more than anyone else, minus being super manipulative.

"I'm all ears."

"It's simple. If Merlot or I aren't here to run things, we'd prefer you over Nebbiolo." She tilted her head, curving her lips sideways in this all-knowing look, as if he should have been able to piece that all together. "You're more responsible. Have more interest in knowing the ins and outs of the way we're doing things. Changing things. Nebbiolo is still acting like we should run the sale of our wines like we all did when we worked for a major distributor. It doesn't work that way."

"That's not entirely true, and you know it. He has good ideas and we should be incorporating some of them."

"Come on, Noir. We are. When there's something you think we should be doing, you speak up, loud and clear. When you're wishy-washy or don't agree, you shut down. Or like the last meeting we had, you argued with Nebbiolo. That man is more stubborn than any of us put together. I might look like Mom and act like Mom most days, but he's bullheaded, just like her, and can sometimes be underhanded."

Noir laughed. "You're right on all counts."

"I'm always right, something my husband is finally accepting." She winked.

"Toby's such a great guy. I'm so happy for you." He squeezed his baby sister's knee. "You've become an amazing woman. Mother to your own little girl and to TJ. I'm sometimes in awe of you."

"Aww, aren't you sweet." She smiled. "How are things with Tamsyn?"

"They're good." He nodded. "I really appreciate

everyone in this family being so accepting of her—and our relationship."

"You thought we wouldn't?"

He laughed. "Because of the rumors, I considered the possibility."

"Dad put those to bed when we were small children. He made it very clear to us what was true and wasn't. We might have been young, especially me, but I got it and I tried to be nice to Tamsyn, only she didn't want much to do with any of us."

"It wasn't that." Nebbiolo was the only person who knew anything about his ongoing friendship with Tamsyn. He'd never shared it with anyone, except his father, but even his dad hadn't known the extent of it. "She was raised in an environment of contradictions. She had a mom whom no one valued. Elizabeth was treated far worse than our mother ever was, and she never could stick up for herself. Then Tamsyn went to live with Fred and Anna. Fred caves to whatever Anna wants and Anna hates our family."

"Well, she hates Mom, and she tolerates the rest of us." Zinny put the straw between her lips, sucking down the last drop.

"In middle school, I started chatting with Tamsyn. We kept it all secret because of all the insanity. But we've been friends forever. It wasn't that she didn't want to be friends with any of us, but she felt as though she couldn't have any friends in this town. That she couldn't trust anyone.

She almost didn't stick around. She had applied for positions at five other police departments, but she wanted to be feel close to her mom and have access to local files."

"I heard it had all been about finding clues to what happened to her mom." Zinny arched a brow.

"That played a big part in her decision," Noir said. "And I'm glad she stayed."

"You make for a cute couple. I'm happy for you. I hope this town isn't too hard on you."

"Noir? Are you back here?" their mother's voice cut through the air, landing on his ears like scalding hot water.

He locked gazes with his sister. "That tone doesn't sound good," he whispered. "I'm in my office."

"Didn't she have a meeting with the Holiday Showcase committee today, which includes Anna?"

Noir nodded just as his mother stepped into the office he shared with Nebbiolo. "Hey, Mom. What's up?"

"If it wasn't only three in the afternoon, I'd start drinking." With her usual dramatic flair, she flung herself on the chair in the corner and scooted in toward the desk. "That woman is going to bring out a side of me that I promised your father would remain in the vault."

Zinny laughed. "Are we referring to Mrs. Cummings or someone else?"

"She was actually tame, compared to Anna today, but Mrs. Cummings agreed and nodded with everything that Anna said." His mom let out a long breath. "Noir, can I speak freely in front of Zinny?"

"Of course. I want no more secrets in this family." The irony that he'd kept his relationship locked up tight for the last month hadn't been lost on him, but moving forward, everything needed to be out in the open if they had any chance of making a real go at it.

"Are you sure Tamsyn's going to be okay with it?" his mom asked.

"She is," he said.

"Anna followed through with her threat, showing everyone on the committee the supposed note she got from Elizabeth shortly before she disappeared." His mom dug into the pocket of her oversized dress. "I managed to get her to print it out, but she's not aware that your dad made copies."

"I'm a little lost in this conversation." Zinny took the note in her hands. Her eyes shifted as she read it. "Elizabeth could be referencing anyone in this note."

"It might not even be by Elizabeth," his mom said. "According to your father, he's not sure that ever made it into the original police file." She shifted her gaze to Noir. "He'd like to ask Tamsyn if she's okay with him doing a comparison of her mother's handwriting for authenticity, along with asking her specifically if she's seen it."

"I want to be there for that conversation," Noir said. "I don't want Tamsyn to feel cornered or defensive in any way."

"I totally understand." His mom nodded.

"What does this have to do with the Holiday Showcase?" Zinny asked.

"Oh, she and Mrs. Cummings were trying to cause problems, removing it from my hands. They got their vote. It's going to be at the winery. They left quite pissed off and said this wasn't the end of it. Unfortunately, I believe Anna made a beeline for the cottage."

"Fucking wonderful," Noir muttered. That was the last thing that Tamsyn needed before heading to her parents' for dinner. He rose, making his way into the hallway, and peeked out the window. Sure enough, Anna's vehicle was next to Tamsyn's patrol car. He contemplated racing to his new home, but that might be perceived as over the top. Instead, he shot Tamsyn a text, letting her know that he was available if she needed backup. He strolled back into his office, setting his cell on his desk.

"What's their relationship really like?" his mother asked, holding up her hand. "I'm not asking for any other reason than I care about you and the position that you're in as her boyfriend."

He rubbed the back of his neck, contemplating his answer. "She's closer to Fred. They have more in common."

"Fred used to stand up to Anna more," his mom said. "But that changed over the years. Your father and I were talking about that earlier. About how it seemed like the shift happened shortly before Elizabeth disappeared. We wondered if it had to do with the fact that Fred also tried to help Elizabeth and it pissed Anna off."

"This note indicates that Elizabeth and Anna were friends." Zinny handed the note back to their mother.

"Can I have a copy of that?" Noir asked.

"You can keep that one." His mom folded it and set it on the desk. "The thing is, Elizabeth and Anna were never friendly. Not back when we were kids, and not as adults, at least that your dad and I ever saw. Fred's a different story. He's a police officer. He has a different temperament, and he needs to not only command respect, but he needs to give it. While he arrested Anna a couple of times, he was lenient and compassionate. He wanted to see her get help so the State didn't come in and take Tamsyn from her. And let me tell you, that nearly happened a few times." His mom took his hand. "The rumor mill about who Tamsyn's father is rearing its ugly head isn't what concerns me for the two of you. It's the mystery of Elizabeth's disappearance that will keep me awake at night. People in this town can be mean. We all know that."

"Tamsyn is insanely sorry for accusing you of having anything to do with what happened to her mom," Noir said.

"She's a young girl who lost her mother. She lashed out at someone who had a fight with her in the middle of town. I don't blame that poor child for anything. But Anna threw that in my face in front of the entire committee, reminding them of that accusation, putting the thought in their head that I could have killed her, and she'll keep doing that. I'm lucky that no one else on the committee believed a single word. However, you know how some people in this town can be, and Anna left ranting that she'll make sure everyone remembers that I had a beef with Elizabeth." His mother let out a long, exasperated, dramatic sigh. "I cared about Elizabeth, but I was angry at what she did. I wanted her to stop. It was hurting my family. But I could have gone about getting my point across differently. I will regret that argument for the rest of my life."

Zinny hopped off the desk, tossing her empty drink in the trash. She squeezed their mother's shoulder. "We don't know why Elizabeth decided to lie about Daddy. You had a right to be angry. No one can fault you for that."

"But I didn't need to get in her face like that," his mom said. "In front of her daughter or the entire town for that matter. It was a delicate situation and your father warned me about letting my emotions get the better of me, which is exactly what happened."

It was rare that his mother took ownership of her actions, but when she did, she did it big. Noir appreciated that about his mom. "We're going in circles," he said. "Maybe I can find something out when I see Tamsyn before we head to her folks' tonight, and again at dinner."

His mom rose, taking his hand. "I'm glad you found

someone to share that lovely heart of yours. I'm thrilled it's Tamsyn because we've seen how she makes your eyes light up. I just hope all this doesn't put the kind of pressure on a new relationship that ends up tearing you apart, because that would break my heart."

"Thanks, Mom." He gave her a big hug. They hadn't always been warm and cuddly. However, in moments like these, he desired that affection. He'd waited a lifetime to feel as though he fit in with his own family, so he wasn't going to let go.

Tamsyn

Tamsyn wiped the foggy mirror with a dry towel. She snagged her hairbrush and worked it through her thick, tangled strands. She stared at herself, wishing the bags under her eyes weren't so prominent. She hadn't slept as well as she would have liked. When she did manage to doze off, she dreamed of her mother and they weren't good dreams. They were riddled with past pains, worries, and feelings of abandonment.

The story of her life.

She pulled open the medicine cabinet, hoping to find something to put under her eyes. Noir had mentioned he'd brought over everything of hers from his old place. There should be some eye cream. But if he'd missed it, perhaps Zinny had left something behind.

Rummaging around the shelves, she found a small box that looked vaguely familiar. She lifted it, examining it in the light. "Where have I seen this before?" she whispered. Her eyes widened as she lifted the top. "Oh my God. No." She thumbed her mother's necklace. The one her mother treated as though it was worth a million dollars.

Tears filled Tamsyn's eyes as she tentatively touched the feather pendant. Her mom had told her that necklace had been a gift from Tamsyn's father. Her mother rarely wore it. Only on special occasions, which seldom happened. After her mother had been declared missing, the police had gone through her mom's things. Fred and Anna had offered a few things of value, but the necklace had never been found.

"No. No. No." The necklace might have belonged to someone else. It could have been mass produced. She closed the box, yanked open the bathroom door, and raced to the middle of the only room. She did a three-sixty. Where the fuck could she hide it until she could do some old-fashioned police work to find out who it actually belonged to?

Noir wasn't a nosy man. He didn't go through her things, but she'd never been secretive either, telling him to leave her stuff alone. The only thing he never touched was her uniform and her weapon.

She stuffed the box into her workbag. It was

unlikely that Noir would ever go in there. But if he did, she'd have some explaining to do. She'd told him about that necklace many times and how much it would have meant to her to have that one thing from her mom.

A tap at the door startled her and she fell over on her butt. She jumped to her feet and smoothed down the front of her jeans. Noir had promised his family wouldn't show up unannounced. She had no right to be angry. This was their property, but still, annoyance bubbled in the center of her chest. She pulled back the door, ready to give whoever was on the other side a piece of her mind.

She gasped, staring at Anna. "What are you doing here?"

Anna barged inside. "I just had the most god-awful meeting. Weezer is a horrible person. You have to break up with Noir. It's for your own good."

"By all means. Come in." She closed the door. "And I'm not doing that. I'm sorry that you had a bad afternoon, but that showcase had nothing to do with me and Noir."

"Are you kidding me?" Anna tossed her purse on the small table, plopping herself on the sofa. She stared at the unmade bed and audibly groaned. "Of all the men in this town, you have to be sleeping with him."

"What happened, Anna?" Quickly, Tamsyn pulled the covers over the bed, fluffing the pillows and placing them against the headboard. She sat on the corner and waited for Anna to open her big mouth.

"Weezer has most of the committee members snowed. The Holiday Showcase is going to be held at the winery. I couldn't prevent that from happening, but I'm hoping to talk some sense into you before this family breaks your heart, because that's what will happen." She leaned forward. "Why can't you see that? Why can't you see that I care about you? Love you like my own. I only want what's best for you, and it's not Noir River."

Tamsyn had planned on having this conversation with Anna and Fred. She thought that having Fred present might defuse the situation. But given how hot Anna came in, there was no time like the present. Besides, Anna might not be so forthcoming if Noir sat at the dinner table. "Why do you hate the River family so much? What did they ever do to you?"

"I don't hate them," Anna said. "But they are manipulative and liars. The whole lot of them. History has told us that. Weezer's family stole that winery." Anna raised her finger and waggled it. "That's a fact. They allowed a doctor to sell babies right under everyone's noses in this town. Carter helped Talbot and her mother fake their own deaths. That's criminal, and yet they are seen as heroes. The things that they have done to their own children." She made a clucking noise with her mouth. "It amazes me that they were able to get them to forgive Weezer and they have all returned home as if nothing had happened. But mark my words, the shit will hit the fan, and I don't want you—my precious little girl —to get caught in the crossfire. You've suffered enough in your life."

"What goes on in their family is none of our business." Tamsyn knew the history. She'd followed it. Studied it. Heard it from Noir and from everyone in this town. The stories were all slightly different, and depending on who told it, the spin was either damning or supportive. Now that Tamsyn had some personal insight into the River family—seen and heard their perspective—she understood their mistakes. Their shame. Their regrets. And how they had done their best to make right all the wrongs.

They were good people who had done their best to survive under the most outrageous situations. Some were their fault; others were the sins of the past.

Either way, they didn't deserve such hatred.

"This feels like you have a personal axe to grind and I want to know what it is," Tamsyn said. "Please tell me so I can understand. Did something in the past happen between you and Weezer? Something that hurt you and now you're holding on to that so tightly it's spilling over on to me?"

"What kind of lies is that family filling your pretty little head with?" Anna rose. She planted her hands on her hips and glared. It was the same look she'd given Tamsyn the day she found out Tamsyn wanted to go to the police academy. Tamsyn had been so excited. She thought both Fred and Anna would be so happy she'd decided to follow in Fred's footsteps and serve their community.

But not Anna.

She thought Tamsyn would be better served getting a degree in something like communications. Or anything outside of law enforcement. She wanted Tamsyn to find a suitable husband and pump out *grandbabies*. While Fred and Anna had raised her, and she'd always be grateful for that, she wasn't sure about having her children call them Grandma and Grandpa.

Maybe Grandma Anna and Grandpa Fred. That might be more appropriate.

Tamsyn wanted to keep her mother's spirit alive, and if and when she did have children, Elizabeth would be their grandmother. She would raise her children in the memory of her mother. Her real mother. That was something she believed she needed to do. Not only for her mother, but for herself and her child. If she ever had one.

"It's not personal, except for the fact it now includes you." Anna dropped her hands to her sides. "I love you. Why can't you see that everything I do is for you?"

"Anna." Tamsyn stood, inching closer, taking Anna's hands. "I need you to accept Noir. I need you to drop this vendetta against the River family. I don't want to be at odds with you."

"How can you forget and forgive all the horrible things that woman did and said to your mother?" Anna palmed her cheek. "You were there. You saw it. I know you remember. And Weezer is capable of anything. Trust me on that."

"My mother did a horrible thing in accusing Carter of being my father. I would probably do the same thing that Weezer did. It was twenty years ago. They are not part of the mystery surrounding what happened to my mom, something I'm still searching for answers to. Please, let this go and get to know Noir. He's a good man, and he cares deeply for me. He's coming to dinner tonight and I want this to be a good thing for all of us. Can you be nice to him? For me? For us? For the sake of our family?" Tamsyn choked out the last word, but she hoped it might be the thing that turned the corner with Anna. She realized she was never going to get Anna to admit anything about her past with Weezer. There was no point in pushing that anymore. It was time to change tactics and she really wanted peace. Needed it for the sake of her relationship with Noir.

And with Anna and Fred.

Noir was the man she wanted to build a life with and regardless of the distance she felt with Anna, she was still the woman who opened her home to her when she had no one. It was worth fighting for.

"Fine." Anna let out a sigh. "I will be on my best behavior tonight and I promise I will give that young man a chance. But it's going to be difficult for Weezer and me to come to any kind of agreement on this. I'm sure she's filling that boy with all sorts of lies about us. And maybe you."

"Rest assured, she's not. Noir's family is quite supportive of us." Tamsyn smiled.

"Maybe to your face. However, they are..." Anna squared her shoulders. "I will work on this. I promise. But don't say I didn't warn you."

That was the best she was going to get and she knew it. "Thank you, Anna. That means a lot to me." She leaned in and kissed Anna's cheek to drive the point home.

Anna wrapped her arms around Tamsyn and hugged her tight.

Affection wasn't something that came easily to Tamsyn, but it was time to accept her place in the world. Anna and Fred had given her a second chance. They deserved to be part of her life. One that included Noir.

7

TAMSYN

Tamsyn squeezed Noir's hand as they walked into the local Italian restaurant in the center of town. Ever since they had made their relationship public, the response had been a mixed bag.

Noir smiled at the hostess. "I have a reservation for two."

"Yes, Mr. River. Please follow me," the hostess, a young girl named Tiffany, said. She shifted her gaze between him and Tamsyn. Her smirk conveyed the rumor mill had yet to die down.

A few heads turned as they strolled past tables to back of the establishment. All the way in the back. The table was tucked in the corner. The worst seat in the house. Tamsyn had noted they passed eight open tables, including the one that his parents had often ate at near the picture window. The same one Noir had promised. Everyone coveted it when they came to this particular restaurant.

"Your waiter will be Aton. He'll be with you in a few minutes," Tiffany said.

"Excuse me," Noir said. "This is not the table I reserved." He pointed. "I'd like to be seated over there where Tamsyn and I can enjoy the snowy view and all the Christmas decorations."

"Noir, it's okay," Tamsyn whispered. The last thing she wanted to do was draw more attention to herself.

"No. It's not," he said behind a tight jaw.

"I'm sorry. We're full tonight and have some important guests—"

"Tiffany." Noir pulled out his cell. "I spoke with Tom. He assured me that I could have the table my father and mother always reserved. They were going to have that one tonight but gave it up because of the Holiday Showcase planning. Now, seat me and my girlfriend over there, or I'll call your boss."

Tamsyn bit her tongue. Noir didn't generally toss his weight around as a River. As a matter of fact, there was a time where he preferred not to be associated with his family. He carried some shame from being called a bastard his entire life, something she could relate to.

"I wasn't aware your folks canceled their reservation." Tiffany frowned. "In that case, you may have the table." She turned on her heel and marched off, not bothering to seat them.

"This is fun," Tamsyn muttered as he tugged her toward the front of the restaurant. "We should have just ordered in." For the most part, people in town were kind. Many congratulated her on her newfound relationship status and told her what a catch Noir was.

That always made her chuckle. Why wasn't she the catch?

"It's ridiculous, is what it is." He pulled out a chair, helping her into it. "My father and Fred had put the rumor to rest last week the first time we went out in public. No one should be staring at us anymore. I have a mind to stick my tongue out and act like a toddler."

"People like to gossip. Although—and this makes me a bitch—I thought having Nix Wilde back in town with what happened to her onstage and her hearing loss would be the thing that took the focus off us."

"I feel really bad for what happened to her and her career." Noir lifted the menu and smiled. He turned it, tapping his finger and the fine selection from The River Winery.

"I love her music. She was so talented," Tamsyn said.

"I'm sure she still is. She has to find a new way to fit into the music business and I have faith that she will. She's a strong woman." He laughed. "When we were kids, Nebbiolo had such a massive crush on her it was hilarious. When her first album came out, he stood in line for hours to get it. Then he plastered our room with posters of her. We teased him relentlessly."

"I wouldn't kick Nix out of bed." Tamsyn raised her water glass.

"I'm not sure what to do with that statement."

Tamsyn winked. Banter with Noir had always been exciting. There was an ease to their relationship that she hadn't experienced before, even amid all this craziness. "I saw her in town with Ford yesterday. Didn't they have a thing back in the day?"

"I believe they did."

Aton appeared at the table. "As I live and breathe," he said. "Noir. It's good to see you. It's been a while."

Noir stretched out his arm. He'd gone to high school with Aton. They weren't friends, but they had been friendly enough, at least from what Tamsyn remembered. "How are things? How's the family?"

"My wife's pregnant again. This will be our second." Aton waggled two fingers. "We're quite excited."

"Congratulations," Tamsyn said. "Give my best to Bennett."

Aton's wife had graduated with Tamsyn. She'd been a quiet girl. Smart, pretty, but not popular because she lived on the wrong side of the tracks, and she'd been poor. Dirt poor. So poor that her parents often had to send her to school with bread and butter for lunch. That was it. Tamsyn knew what it was like to be on the outs with the entire town and did her best to be kind to Bennett. It was nice to see her and Aton carving out a little piece of happiness for themselves.

"So, you two are a couple now." Aton smiled. "That's causing quite the stir in this town. Sorry about Tiffany. I filled her in on the facts. She shouldn't have treated you that way. Personally, I'm happy for the two of you. Now, what can I start you off with?"

"How about a bottle of Eliza Jane's newest blend and pair that with this cheese platter." Noir tapped the menu.

"That's perfect," Aton said. "That wine is selling like bananas. Everyone is raving about it."

"That's good to know." Noir set his menu aside and stared at Tamsyn with adoring eyes.

She would never tire of the way Noir treated her with kindness and respect.

"I have to admit it's weird having Anna be so nice to me and she's even being agreeable to my mom," Noir said.

The front door opened and Noir's father strolled inside. He didn't bother making small talk with Tiffany; he marched right over to Noir's table. "Sorry to interrupt your dinner." His dad pulled out a chair and made himself comfortable. "We need to talk."

"It's never good when you start a conversation like that," Noir said.

"Should I excuse myself?" Tamsyn asked. Sometimes his family could come in hot and anyone involved with their children needed to know when to exit gracefully. A skill Tamsyn had yet to master.

"Nope. This involves you, unfortunately." Carter let out a long breath.

Aton stepped up to the table with a bottle of wine and two glasses. "Oh. Hello, Mr. River. Shall I get you a glass?"

"Yes, please," Carter said. "I'm going to need a bit of alcohol."

"I'll be right back." Aton set the two glasses down, along with the bottle and scurried off.

"Dad, what's going on?" Noir asked. "If it's so important, why didn't you have us come home?"

"I'd like to know that too." Tamsyn fiddled with her napkin. The last time Carter River needed to down some alcohol where she had been concerned, was when she'd accused Weezer of killing her mother. That had been one hell of a chat. One that ended with Tamsyn understanding more about her mom than she wanted to.

"I didn't want to risk anything being in a text string." Carter reached across the table, snagging the wine and corkscrew, opening the bottle himself.

"Oh, no, sir. Let me do that for you," Aton said as he set the third glass on the table.

"No worries, Aton. I've got it." Carter poured most of the bottle into the wineglasses. "Thanks." Carter was mostly a patient man. He could wait for the right opportunity to do almost anything. The sense of urgency palpating from his skin was completely unnerving, and it took a lot to rattle Tamsyn.

Aton was a good waiter and knew when it was time to disappear, and he did just that.

"I'm going to talk, and you two are going to listen." Carter turned his attention to Tamsyn. "Especially you. When I'm finished, we'll go over the legalities of everything."

"Dad—"

"Quiet, son." Carter took a hearty sip. "You remember how we installed a new security system last year?"

Noir nodded.

"Well, someone tampered with it. I know this because one of the cameras on west side of the vineyard was disabled a couple of days ago. I wasn't sure if it was a glitch or something else."

"What do you mean, disabled? And how do you know someone tampered with it?" Tamsyn found it difficult to shut off the cop side of her brain. A hazard of the job.

Carter ran a hand over his face. "At first, it seemed like something happened to the camera. That it just went offline, as if it had malfunctioned, so I had a new one installed and everything is up and running. But something didn't sit right with me or the company that runs the security at the winery."

"What did you find?" Tamsyn leaned forward.

"The system isn't overly complicated. It's a bunch of motion sensors that once tripped, activate the cameras that only record once motion is detected. Because the wind can set those suckers off, we check them, then allow the system to tape over them. We got notice that one went off. Shortly after, it went offline, but when we checked the video, we didn't see anything. However, because the company concluded neither the camera nor sensors were defective, they did a deep dive and found footage of a trespasser on the winery."

"Have you called my office?" Tamsyn asked.

"Not yet," his father said. "This is where it gets tricky because I can't prove anything."

"What do you mean?" Noir asked. "You have an image of someone on the property. That's conclusive evidence."

"Tamsyn, I'm trusting you to be a member of this family for a few moments, and not a cop. Can you do that?" Carter cocked his head. "If you can't, now is the time to excuse yourself."

"That's a lot to ask of me, Carter." She leaned back and glanced at the ceiling. Carter had always been a fair and reasonable man. There had to be something so compelling that he was asking for her to suspend her duties as an officer. "State the bare bones and I'll tell you if I need you to stop."

"That's fair enough." Carter nodded.

Noir folded his arms across his chest and glared.

"Whoever trespassed obviously didn't know where all the new cameras were, so we only see them coming onto the property. We don't even see them leaving. But when I went to the area in question and did a search, I found something. Someone dug up the earth and planted something on my property. I know without a doubt it wasn't there before. I didn't look too deep, but it will make this family—specifically, my wife—look suspect. The thing is, I don't know if it's a bona fide clue to something that could possibly give Tamsyn answers. If it is, it could lead to something really bad for this family because of where it was found and that means someone is fucking with us."

"That's cryptic." Tamsyn held Noir's stare. A million things ran through her head, but it landed on one thing.

His eyes grew wide with recognition of what his father's words could mean. It all had to come back to her mother; otherwise, Carter wouldn't have included her at all.

"Would you like me to be more specific?" Carter asked. "Because I'm not sure I want to do that sitting here."

"No. I think this is a good place to stop," Tamsyn said. "I need to chew on that for a moment before I decide what to do next."

"You're joking, right?" Noir rested his elbows on the table. "You're not going to ask probing questions? Get more details? Ask for specifics?"

"I need to consider the position I'm being put in." Tamsyn lifted her glass and sipped. "I have too much information as it is. I should act as a police officer. So, if I do start asking those questions, no one is going to like what I do next. I need to roll this around in my mind for a moment and decide if I can do what your father is asking and set aside my responsibilities as a cop. That's no easy task."

"Why don't we enjoy this wine, eat some cheese, and then go back to the winery. I'm willing to share everything with both of you, but Tamsyn, right now, this is not a police matter. It's something I stumbled upon."

"Whether you stumbled upon it or not, I will decide what is actually a police matter and what we can keep private," Tamsyn said. "I'll wait to hold my judgment until I get a good look at what you uncovered."

"I was afraid you were going to say that," his father said. "But it's a risk I'm willing to take." He nodded. "I believe I owe it to you to give you the first look."

"I hate being in the dark." Noir downed half his drink. "How bad is it?"

"By itself, it's not horrible. But I don't think this will end here," Carter said. "I believe someone is out to get your mother, and this is only the beginning."

"It's not the first time someone has come at Weezer," Tamsyn said. "She's always managed to come out on top."

"My mother is inherently a good person. She's done some dumb things in the past, but it's all been about protecting her family. People don't see her decisions the same way we do. They see the lies and manipulations," Noir said. "I can't say that some of them haven't hurt. However, I can't imagine that anyone would come at her so hard as to... well, I don't know because my father isn't telling us everything."

"Let me put it to you this way, son. No good deed goes unpunished." His dad cocked a brow. "And when your mom and I do one, everyone thinks we have an ulterior motive. This one had a ripple effect that no one understands. Much like what I did for Talbot and her mother and it's about to bite this family in ways that we've never seen before."

Tamsyn

Tamsyn stood at the edge of the River Winery property. The moonlight cut through the darkness like a big flashlight shining bright. Puffy white snowflakes floated from the sky, dancing in front of her eyes.

"What the fuck, Carter." Tamsyn rubbed her chest where it met her neck. As a little girl, her mom would let her try on the feather pendant necklace. Her mother would tell her how beautiful it looked on her and how one day it would be hers, when the time was right. When her father claimed her as his own.

Tamsyn's fingertips burned. "What's under that pile

of leaves and dirt? And don't tell me you didn't look, because I can tell you did."

"It's fresh and it wasn't there a week ago." Carter pulled his jacket tight. His nonanswer didn't help Tamsyn's growing concern. Or calm her racing pulse.

She took three steps back. "I don't want anyone coming any closer." She paced out the size of what appeared to be a shallow grave, noting where it had been disturbed, indicating someone had peered inside, but the recent snowfall helped cover those tracks. "I need some honest answers, Carter." She glanced between Noir and his father.

Noir stood four feet to her left. He hadn't moved since they arrived. His hands were stuffed in his pockets, his forehead crinkled.

"I don't have any," Carter said.

"Bullshit." Tamsyn inched closer, bending down, examining the area that had appeared to have been recovered. She found a stick and moved the ground around, careful not to disturb too much. A million thoughts shot through her brain. Brooklyn's alpaca farm was located to the north. The access road looped between the two properties at this point. It was owned by the winery but gave Brooklyn the ability to access the river from the south end. Carter had created the road when he and Weezer took over ownership of the winery as a courtesy. They were kind and generous that way.

But Brooklyn and Caleb would never bury an animal

on the River property, much less go to the trouble of taking out one of the security cameras. They had wanted the added security as much as the River family.

"Talk to me, Carter," Tamsyn said.

"Are you a cop or my son's girlfriend?" Carter asked.

"Both." There was no way Tamsyn could let this sit and not call it in. The only question became when and how she chose to deal with it.

"Dad. Why are you being so sketchy about this? What happened that you aren't telling us?" Noir took a hand out of his pocket and took off his cap. He adjusted it, brushing off the snow, then put it back on.

"Your mother received an anonymous email earlier today," Carter said. "It wasn't threatening in nature, which is why we didn't think too much about it."

"What did it say?" Tamsyn asked.

"Whoever sent it told Weezer her past was going to catch up to her and she wasn't going to be able to run from it or manipulate the outcome this time." Carter turned and made his way to the fence. He leaned against the post. "I know how the law works. Anything I say to you can be used against us, but I have a gut feeling about what's in that grave."

"Why? What did you see when you pushed aside those leaves and some of the dirt?"

"Bones," Carter said. "And I know human remains when I see them."

"Jesus, Dad." Noir raced to his father's side. "Why would someone bring a body to our property?"

"You both know I have to call this in." Tamsyn pulled out her cell. "I will need that email, the video footage, and any other piece of evidence you have. Is there anything else you're leaving out?"

Carter glanced down.

"Fuck," Tamsyn muttered. "Spit it out before the rest of my colleagues get here."

"A couple of days ago, Weezer was cleaning the dining room and she found a small box that had been stuffed in the back of the china cabinet. It wasn't ours and she had no idea where it came from or when it was put there." Carter caught her gaze. "When we opened it, we didn't recognize most of the items, until we came across one thing."

"What was that?" Noir asked.

Carter ran a hand across his face. "A charm bracelet that Weezer had given to Elizabeth when Tamsyn was born."

"You've got to be fucking kidding me." An image of the feather pendant necklace flashed before Tamsyn's eyes. "You should have called me the second you found it. I'm sure your fingerprints are all over it now."

"You're right about that." Carter sighed.

"That box wasn't there six months ago," Noir said. "I know that because we all helped Mom clean that out. Zinny took some wineglasses. Chablis took Grandma's old china set, and Merlot and Talbot took the tea set."

"Anyone besides family there to prove that?"

Tamsyn swallowed the thick bile that filled her throat. Her gaze shifted to the shallow grave.

Human remains.

Her mother.

It couldn't be.

But every bone in her body told her it was.

"It was a family affair," Carter said. "Every member was there. But no one outside of my children, their spouses, and my grandchildren." He lifted his hand. "I do have photographs from that day. Pictures of the items. Images of us cleaning out that cabinet, among other things."

"That will be helpful. I'll need your phone, or anyone else's who has pictures of that day. I need time-stamps. Anything that can help show you emptying out that cabinet, but to be honest, that won't be enough." Tamsyn's finger hovered over her phone. "I'm recommending that neither of you or anyone in your family say another word to me. Call your lawyer."

"That would be me," Carter said.

"That's not a good idea, and you know it." She tapped Fred's number. "While I don't see a crime, if there is a human body in that grave, and it's who we think it is, we all know where this investigation is going to point."

"That's a bit premature, don't you think?" Noir ripped off his snow-covered cap and stuffed it in his pocket. His face hardened and he stared at her with daggers shooting from his eyes.

For a split second, she contemplated telling them about her mother's pendant, but thought better of it for the moment.

"I'm looking out for your family," she said, pointing to the grave. "This is new." She waved her hand toward the fence. "I can tell that was cut and tied back together. With the amount of snow coming down, it's going to be hard to find footprints and tire tracks, so time is not on your side. However, the State forensics team will be able to tell if this body has been here for a while or put here recently. That will tell us a lot. In the meantime, protecting the integrity of this scene is my job. Your job is to protect your family and that starts by understanding that none of this looks good on the outside, looking in."

"You're acting as if someone in my family did something wrong," Noir said.

"No. I'm behaving like a cop. Now let me do my job." She hit Fred's number and turned.

"She's right," Carter said. "I knew what would happen the second I brought her out here. I've already contacted Ben Hargrove."

"Your buddy from law school?" she heard Noir ask.

"Yes. He's on his way," Carter said. "I could have called the police first, but that wouldn't have been fair to Tamsyn. I thought she should have been the first person to see this. Your mother and I owed her that."

Tamsyn closed her eyes for a brief second. A single cold tear dribbled down her cheek. Carter had always been a kind and gentle soul. While he put his family first, he took care of the people of this town, herself included. She appreciated what he had tried to do and the sentiment behind it, but in this case, it could end up backfiring on him and his wife.

8

NOIR

Noir sat at the island in the small kitchen, staring into a cup of coffee. The steam rose toward his face, carrying a rich aroma. It filled his senses, awakening his brain, but did nothing to settle his nerves. Those were like bricks in the pit of his stomach that won't move.

He'd given a statement to Fred, Tamsyn, Eddy, and a police officer from the State with Ben present. It had been short and sweet. Nothing had been asked or answered that he believed could jeopardize his family, but he still didn't like the way Tamsyn carried herself. It was as if she were a different person.

As if she were anyone other than the woman he loved.

He'd seen her in action before, but this hurt his heart. It felt like a personal assault and he couldn't separate his girlfriend from the police officer doing her job.

He and his parents had left the scene around midnight. His father had told him to go home and get some sleep. That hadn't happened. Every time he closed his eyes, all he could focus on was what might have been buried in the ground.

Glancing at his cell, he checked the time and for messages.

It was five in the morning and he hadn't heard shit from Tamsyn.

He sipped his coffee. It burned the roof of his mouth and soured his belly. He had half a mind to march off into the vineyard and find out what the hell was going on, but he knew not only would that do no good, but she'd send him away.

Lights cut through the darkness, flashing through the window. His heart lurched to his throat. A combination of anger, fear, and sadness filled his soul.

Anger over the situation.

Fear regarding what could be happening with all the different scenarios that played out in his mind.

And horrible sadness for a conclusion that would rock Tamsyn's world.

And his.

He raced to the front door, swinging it open.

Tamsyn stepped from Fred's patrol car. She hugged him.

Fred waved but said nothing before ducking back behind the steering wheel.

Noir wasn't sure if that was good or bad. He held the door open.

Tamsyn kicked her snowy boots on the step. Shaking off her coat, she handed it to him and stepped inside. She sucked in a deep breath as she made her way toward the kitchen. She pulled out a mug and placed it under the coffee maker. "Did you get any sleep?"

"A few minutes here and there," he said. "Are they done?"

"No." She sat at the island and palmed the cup. "The State's CSI team has taken over the removal of the remains."

"So, it's definitely a human body."

"I shouldn't be talking to you about this." She kept her gaze firmly planted on her beverage. "I'm sorry. But unless you have information to give me, or I have something to inform you about—officially—discussing an ongoing investigation that involves your family would be inappropriate." She tilted her head. "Even if we don't believe anyone had anything to do with it. I'd lose my job."

"It's not the first time you haven't been able to share with me parts of your job." He joined her at the island, sitting close, but in the six weeks they'd been sharing a bed, he'd never felt further apart.

"That's true, but this is different and honestly, I don't like it."

He laughed, but it wasn't a funny one. "I can't say I do either."

"The worst part is Fred is already trying to pull me from having any part of the investigation." When she caught Noir's gaze, tears filled her beautiful eyes. "He was pissed at how I handled the initial call, not understanding Carter put me in that position. Not even when Carter came to my defense. If those remains come back to be my mother's, Fred will make sure my hands don't touch this case."

"I'm pretty sure it has more to do with your relationship with me and my family." He looped his arm around her waist and kissed her cheek. "He's only doing it because he cares about you and I'm sure he'd consider pulling you off even if you weren't dating me."

"That's what he said." She rested her head against Noir's shoulder. "I can't believe this is happening and I want to wring your father's neck. I totally get he thought he was doing me a favor, but in turn, he didn't help himself—or your mom—any."

"They haven't done anything wrong."

She jumped off the chair. "I can't believe I'm going to do this." She went to the closet and pulled out her duffel. "We're going to ignore the fact that I'm a cop right now. I'm talking to you as your girlfriend."

"All right." He arched a brow.

"I found this in the bathroom the morning after you

moved in here." With a shaky hand, she held out a small box.

"What is it?"

"Look inside."

He lifted the top, gasped, and dropped the box as if it were on fire. "Holy shit. Is that your mother's? Because it looks exactly like what you've described. What the hell was it doing in my bathroom?" He glanced to the floor, then back to her. "I thought we weren't going to talk about this?"

"If our relationship is going to work, if I'm going to continue spending most of my nights here, we need to be honest where we can," she said. "I'm not giving it to Fred, the sheriff's office, or the State's team. I know I should. I know all the legalities of not doing it and I've probably lost my motherfucking mind. But my prints are all over it, so it's already been compromised. Not to mention, I don't want to give it up."

"I don't mean to be accusatory, but Anna used the bathroom the night I moved in." The moment the statement left his lips, he realized what a dick move it was, but he stated a fact. Something Tamsyn—as a cop —should appreciate and needed to know.

She narrowed her stare. "What are you suggesting? Anna's a lot of things, but why on earth would she do that? Why would she keep something so precious to me for all these years and then randomly shove it in your medicine cabinet? Especially when all she's ever wanted was to be closer to me. To feel a connection to me. That would be one way to accomplish that."

"I'm sorry, sweetheart. I didn't mean to imply she was trying to harm my family. I'm tired. I'm frustrated. I don't like what's happening to my parents. I'm grasping at straws and Anna hates my mother." He held up his hand. "I mean no disrespect, but if Anna did have that necklace and she had given it to you, it would have driven a bigger wedge. Especially if she had waited any length of time to give it to you."

Tamsyn opened her mouth, but quickly snapped it shut. She shifted her gaze to her coffee. "We're speculating, but I'll agree that could be true," she said. "But let's look at what we do know. Anna and your mom are cruel to each other. They say mean things. Torment one another. Pull stupid stunts over a stupid showcase and other status things in this town. It's been going on for years. Everyone sees it and it's not one-sided. Your mom has done some shitty things to Anna. I could name a few if you want."

"I'm going to be a dick, but Anna showed—"

"Yeah. The note. It was underhanded. Desperate. But I talked to Anna about that. She's sorry and knows it was a bitch move and she shouldn't have done it."

"It doesn't help how my family looks in all this. It goes beyond being cruel. And Anna did it with the sole purpose of putting ideas in everyone's head about your mom's disappearance and my mother's possible role in it. It's defamation, at the very least."

"I understand why you're angry. But if it wasn't that, Anna might have tossed some other transgression in Weezer's face, and they are plentiful." Tamsyn eased into his arms. "That letter could be about anyone. It's actually not relevant in this case," she said.

"Relevant or not, people are talking. You should know better than anyone how the rumor mill works in this town. You've been at the center of it. So has my mom and my entire family. And we've faced it longer and with more scandals than you. I don't know if we can survive another one."

"I've never seen your dad so shaken before. Fred took that as him looking guilty, but the only thing I see Carter as guilty of is being stupid."

"My father is anything but."

"Perhaps, but he should have at least come to me the second he found that box. And he should have called the police and then called us to come to that shallow grave." She glanced up. "Do you think your parents could be keeping other things from me? About this investigation? My mother? Your father's all hot to do DNA stuff with a few potential men who could be my biological father, but that scares me."

"Let him do it," Noir said. "As for the rest of it." He shrugged. "I put nothing past my family. If they truly believe they are protecting you, they will hold it close to the cuff."

"That's not helping."

"I'm being honest," Noir said. "Especially when it

comes to my mother. But my dad? He's a lawyer. He will play that game and you're a cop. You will either work great together, or you will clash. You know how that works." He cupped her face. "Is there anything you can tell me?"

"I love you, Noir. I want us to work. But if I tell you this, can you keep it to yourself?"

He pursed his lips. "I have struggled with my relationships with my siblings and parents because of secrets. I made a promise that when you and I finally came out in the open, there wouldn't be any more."

"Okay, I'll keep this to myself."

"No," Noir said. He swallowed the thick lump in his throat. It tasted like betrayal. But he loved both Tamsyn and his family. He was stuck in the middle. If he knew things his family didn't, he might be able to help them from the sidelines.

And if he had to, he'd break Tamsyn's trust, which would destroy his relationship.

He hoped it wouldn't come down to that.

"I won't tell my family," he said.

"Are you sure? I get I'm asking a lot of you."

"It's fine. I want to know. It will help me understand your position better and that's what's important right now."

"That body hadn't been there very long. It was put there recently. But that doesn't mean your parents are off the hook for anything. Not until forensics come back, and if that is my mother, you know what this town is going to think. And whoever takes lead on this case is going to start in your backyard. I'm going to fight tooth and nail to investigate it and you're not going to like it."

Noir didn't need to be reminded of that one.

Carter

Carter pushed his plate to the center of the table.

"You have to eat something." Weezer shoved the food back in front of him, stabbing some eggs and raising them to his face.

"I'm not hungry." He leaned back, folding his arms defiantly across his chest. "Fred was being a dick. Not just to me, but to Tamsyn. She did nothing wrong."

"Family dynamics, dear. And he's her boss."

"I don't give a shit. I'm the one he should be mad at. Not her. She's stuck between a rock and a hard place because I put her there, and I'm wondering why I did that."

"Because you care about that child. Because you love our son. Same reason we do everything. Doesn't matter if we make the right decision or not, we do it out of love." She rested her hand on his thigh. "And the only thing we did wrong was not taking what we found to Tamsyn sooner."

Carter ran a hand across his unshaven face. "That would have been a mistake too. The only proper choice would have been to call the cops."

"That's exactly what Tamsyn is. A cop."

"She's also the woman our son loves, complicating the shit out of this." He snagged a piece of bacon and plopped it in his mouth. "I knew this town would gossip for ten minutes about their relationship. I figured they would have their whispers, their stares, and then it would go away. I never in a million years thought it would bring out this level of crazy." He took his wife's hand. "We have to tell her the rest of this story. We have to."

"I know, but it has to come from me since I left it out the last time we chatted."

"Actually, it should come from Fred. The fact that our phone conversation with Elizabeth five days after she disappeared never made it into any police report boggles my mind." Carter's stomach growled. He hated being hungry after the night's events. He wanted to tell his body to fuck off. He snagged the fork and shoveled some eggs into his mouth. He refused to taste them.

"It wasn't a conversation. My phone rang. I answered it. I said hello, no one responded back. The call ended. Fred took the information and he wondered if someone could have found the phone. Called a random number in it. Besides, her car and cell were found a day after that at the bus station a few towns over."

"Like I told you then, I find that all too convenient."

"Are you telling me that Fred's pulling something over on us? On Tamsyn? Because you put him in the office of chief of police." Weezer pursed her lips. "He might not have much of a backbone when it comes to Anna, but he's a good cop. A decent man."

"I'm not saying Fred's up to anything. Far from it. What I am saying is that someone is fucking with us and I don't like it."

"Come on, old man. Twenty years later, and they're just now playing the ace up their sleeve? Even I'm not that patient."

"Sweetheart. It's not about being patient. Whoever this is, whether it be the killer or someone else, it's because they're frightened of us. Or frightened of Noir and Tamsyn being together. Like perhaps Tamsyn's real father."

"What would he have to do with anything?" Weezer asked.

"For the last ten years, the only people who had the proof that I wasn't Tamsyn's father was us and Tamsyn. Now that it's out, whoever is her father might not want to be found out. We find that man, and we might know who buried those bones on our vineyard."

"We haven't had this chat in a while, so who are your list of viable suspects and have you done anything about this lately?"

"I asked Tamsyn if she'd be willing to do a couple

more DNA samples." Carter pushed the food around on his plate.

"Did you give her names?"

Carter nodded. "I'd like to start with Richard Berkin."

Weezer whistled. "Whether he slept with Elizabeth or not, I doubt he's going to agree to a paternity test, especially if you ask. He's filed for an appeal and he's screaming to anyone who will listen that we set him up."

"We kind of did." Carter smiled. "And I'm damn proud of that one." He let out a long breath. "During Merlot and Talbot's wedding, I kept studying Talbot and Tamsyn for similarities, and I didn't find any."

"Genetics don't always work that way." Weezer placed her hand over his wrist. "Who else?"

He cocked his head. "The list hasn't changed."

"It helps to talk this through."

"Fine," he said. "Charlie Osborne, Sheriff Boyd Morton, and Michael Kirkpatrick."

"All of them are good prospects. Only, if I had to place a bet, it would be on Michael. When was the last time you heard from him?" Weezer asked.

"Four years ago and the trail is dead. My private investigator can't find him and that means he's most likely using and on the streets again. I hope that's not the case, but that man has had a rough life."

"You've asked Charlie and Boyd to take a paternity

test before, and they both turned you down flat. Do you think you can convince them this time?"

"I'm not going to try." Carter arched a brow. "For years, Tamsyn wanted her father to appear in her life. To want her. She didn't want to force it. If he wanted her, then she'd welcome it. If he didn't, she didn't want him in her life. I want to think she's of the mindset that her biological father could have something to do with what's happening now."

"You believe that, or she told you that? Because those are two very different statements."

Carter lifted his mug, sipping his coffee, wishing he'd made it of the Irish variety. "She didn't come out and say it. She's been acting all cop, working with the sheriff's department and State. But I know that young lady. She's smart and I see the conflict in her eyes. She's walking a fine line between being Noir's girlfriend, supporting us through something that's an obvious setup, and doing her job without compromise."

"That's a shit place to be."

He took Weezer's hand. "I need you to let me handle this. I can't believe I'm going to say this, but please keep your focus on the Holiday Showcase and stay the hell away from this case. Follow whatever the police need, except don't speak to them without me present, including Tamsyn, unless it's social. Got it?"

"And what the hell are you going to do, darling husband?"

"The same thing I always do, protect my family." He took her chin with his thumb and forefinger. "But I mean it, Weezer. Don't meddle. When you do that, you tend to make things worse."

She narrowed her eyes.

Never a good sign.

"I love you with everything that I am. You're brilliant with so many things. This is not one of them. Law, police shit, that's my area. Let me do what I do best."

"I will stay in my lane. I promise." Weezer raised her finger. "But we need to show Tamsyn that text from Elizabeth. And we need to do it sooner rather than later."

"I'll set up that meeting, but you'll do it with me present."

"That's fair and reasonable," Weezer said.

"That's my girl."

Noir waited for his coffee and doughnut, feeling like every pair of eyes in the Green Bean were on him and they were filled with judgment. He took off his cap and stuffed it in his coat pocket. Six inches of fresh snow had fallen since last night. The police had roped off part of the vineyard and the access road. A skeleton CSI team were still out there, doing God only knew what.

"Excuse me," a familiar female voice prickled his ears.

His body stiffened. Alison Token was the last person he wanted to chat with on any given day, but especially today. She'd been stirring up trouble for weeks with her so-called reporting. Interviewing anyone who had an opinion on Tamsyn's missing mother, the activity at the vineyard, and even the controversy over the showcase.

He turned, forcing a smile. "Hello, Alison."

"Noir," she said. "Would you mind giving a statement? On the record. My camera crew is just outside."

"I do mind." He did his best not to tighten all the muscles in his face. He didn't want to give away his anger and frustration, but he did want to get his point across.

"Silence is a strong message. Don't you want to say something about what's happening in your life right now?"

"He gave you your answer, now go away," Caleb Ransom said.

"I wasn't talking to you." Alison planted her hands on her hips.

"I'm not giving any kind of statement." Noir said, snagging his sugary treat and tall coffee.

"Stop gossiping," Caleb said. "Half your story was bogus." Caleb was no stranger to being accused of something he hadn't done. He'd been one of the main reasons Merlot had chosen to become a parole officer in the first place. Even though Caleb had been vindicated, it didn't stop a few idiots in Candlewood Falls from glaring and whispering behind his back.

But today's town grumbling had been all about the morning news regarding the human remains found at The River Winery. Alison even had to mention Tamsyn and Noir's relationship status and the old rumor about her possible connection to the River family. Alison was nice enough to say that rumor was defunct, but she still put it out there for all to judge.

However, Alison went too far when she showed the video of Noir's mother fighting with Elizabeth. It was sensationalism. She did it solely to get the network bigwigs to notice her and for ratings. All it did was create speculation.

And now she sat three tables over with one of the ladies from the hair salon.

Fucking wonderful.

Noir sat across from his brother-in-law Dax, who had been holding the table since the Green Bean was packed. Typical for a winter morning when the patio couldn't be open. He took out his doughnut, setting it on the napkin. His stomach twisted and turned. Tamsyn had to go into the station and fill out a bunch of paperwork. Then she had a meeting with his parents.

That made him nervous as fuck.

After that, all she wanted to do was sleep for ten hours. He couldn't blame her, but at least she was willing to do that in his bed.

"You've been staring at the doughnut for the last five minutes," Dax said. "Are you going to eat it?"

"Would you like it? Because I've lost my fucking appetite." Noir pushed it in front of his brother-in-law. "That witch, Alison, is staring at me like a fucking vulture. She was outside my parents' house this morning. My father pulled his lawyer shit on her, and she left, but she's relentless. The worst part is she barely covered the important part of the story.

As in, someone put human remains on the vineyard."

"That right there has Brooklyn freaked out," Caleb said. "That part of the winery butts right up against the alpaca farm. We told Fred and Tamsyn the night in question, Lucy was going nuts. And that wasn't the only time. We told the police that. However, we did have a problem with raccoons for a bit."

"So did we." Noir lifted the lid of coffee. He inhaled the rich aroma before taking a slow sip.

"Carter and I are going to put up cameras on the access road. I'm also adding more along my side of the fence. We just never have because it felt like we'd be invading Weezer's time with Alpacino."

Noir's lips defied him and he smiled. "I'll never understand her relationship with that animal."

"It is unique, that's for sure." Caleb glanced over his shoulder. "Your dad would probably be pissed if you gave her a statement, wouldn't he?"

"That would be putting it mildly," Noir said.

"We're under strict orders not to speak to the media or the cops without Carter or Ben present," Dax said. "Shit. Don't look now, but here comes Anna."

"Fucking great." Noir reached across the table and snagged the treat he'd given to Dax. He needed something to focus on. He broke off a piece, dunked it in his coffee, and popped it in his mouth. He kept his gaze on the glaze floating in his brew.

"Oh my God. Noir. How are you and your family

holding up?" Anna pushed through the crowd. She stood at the table, clutching that damn oversized bag of hers. "I can't imagine what you must going through. Or feeling. I'd be so freaked out if I found... found... I can't even say it."

Wonderful. Kind and caring Anna. Noir had only seen that side of Anna twice.

When Riesling's ex had taken half the town for their life savings and left her and her daughter high and dry.

And when Chablis' medical records had been compromised and shared with the world.

Outside of that, Anna always stirred the pot and manipulated any situation to get whatever it was she desired, especially if that meant putting his mother in her place.

"We're all fine, thank you." Noir didn't think it would be wise to be anything other than nice with Alison sitting less than ten feet away.

"Fred couldn't get into the details when he got home this morning. I couldn't believe it when I saw the morning news," Anna rambled on. "I tried calling your mom, but she's not answering. I know everyone on the Holiday Showcase committee is so worried about what this will mean. Please tell her to call me back so we can discuss this."

And there you had it. That's all Anna cared about. The stupid fucking showcase. She and Mrs. Cummings were plotting how to have it change venues once again —and it was only a week away.

But that wasn't happening. Not unless the police department shut them down, and then if that happened, it would be canceled for the first time in a hundred years.

"I'm sure she'll return your call as soon as she gets a chance," Noir said. "It's still early in the day and when I left this morning, she was knee-deep in conversations with the staff about the decorations. There's nothing to worry about."

Anna scoffed. "Seriously? There was a grave site found on your property. One that shouldn't be there. I'd say that's cause for concern." Anna hugged her purse. "Maybe I should stop by. Weezer's taking on too much. We can't afford for this showcase—"

"Weezer has it covered," Dax said. "If anyone can tackle this under adversity, it's my mother-in-law."

"I'll second that." Caleb smiled. "We're really looking forward to it this year. It's always so awesome when it's at The River Winery."

Noir appreciated his friends' support, especially now that half the room had shifted their gaze to their table. "I need to get back to work. I'll see you two later." He stood. "Would you like me to give a message to Tamsyn? I'll be seeing her this afternoon." He shouldn't dig at Anna that way, but oh, it felt so good.

She pursed her lips. "No. I will be talking with my daughter later." Anna turned on her heel and marched right back where she came from.

"God, she's exhausting." Noir snagged his coffee. "I

really do need to run. Thanks for hanging out with me for a bit."

"Anytime, man," Caleb said.

Dax glanced at his watch. "I have to get to CWF Prep. I'll walk out with you."

"Worried Anna's going to ambush me outside?"

"More concerned with the fact that Alison started packing up her bag and is now following us," Dax said. "Right to our cars and drive away fast. Do not pass go. Do not collect two hundred dollars."

"I think that statement should be more like: don't get arrested by my girlfriend for saying or doing something stupid."

"That woman certainly is good for you." Dax slapped him on the back. "She kind of reminds me of a cross between Zinny and—well, I'm not sure. But she's got some fire in her belly, and she's a good egg."

"Don't ever compare my girlfriend to my sister again." Noir laughed. "That's just gross."

Tamsyn

Tamsyn wasn't sure what was worse. Being summoned by Fred and Anna.

Or Carter and Weezer.

Both were equally disturbing in different ways

considering Tamsyn's relationship status and the current situation at The River Winery.

She took the glass of wine that Weezer offered and stared at the family portrait hanging over the fireplace that had been taken at Weezer and Carter's second wedding. Everyone, including Talbot and Merlot's son, Corbin, had been there.

"The only person missing from that picture is you," Weezer eased back into the rocking chair.

Tamsyn nearly spit out her wine. She coughed and gagged, hoping nothing came out of her nose. Now that would be truly embarrassing.

"Too early for that?" Weezer smiled.

"A little bit. Plus, a lot is going on."

That wiped the grin right off Weezer's face.

The last thing Tamsyn needed was to piss off anyone in Noir's family, especially his mother. Getting into her good graces felt like nothing short of a miracle.

"We might as well dig into why we asked you to come over before Noir left the winery." Carter sat in front of the mantel. He lifted his glass, swirling the wine, watching the liquid hug the sides. From the outside, he didn't look like a refined man. More like rough around the edges. He always wore jeans. Even in court, unless it was a judge who required a suit, which she'd learned over the years, he hated. He liked his flannel shirts. If it was dressy, he wore a button-down. Sometimes blue, other times pink. Never white. That would be boring, according to him.

In the summertime, it was a black T-shirt. Or a collared golf shirt, but nothing flashy. He didn't do fancy except for his truck. He liked red. For as long as she'd known him, he'd driven a red SUV or pickup. He got a new one every couple of years, stating it was one of the few things he enjoyed spending money on.

Carter River was a bit of an oxymoron. Then again, all of them were. The whole family wasn't what one would expect. They appeared to be one thing on the outside. All tough as nails. And they were. But each one had a softness. A kindness. They were real, genuine people who cared about others, and that had always been the unexpected.

"Is this about me and Noir? Are you worried about how our relationship is going to work or look under the current circumstances?" she asked.

"No," Carter said quickly. "We went through the wringer with Toby and Zinny. That could have turned out ten shades of bad."

"I'll never forget the comment she made about Officer Bob in court," Tamsyn said.

"I forgot you were working the courthouse during that case." Carter stretched out his legs. "Zinny certainly doesn't pull any punches. But she and Toby survived that entire ordeal. They're married. She's going to legally adopt TJ. They have a child of their own. It's all good. I'm only worried about the toll any of this will take on you and Noir. I don't want to see either of you get hurt."

"So far, the worst of it's been from idiots who aren't strapped with the correct history. Thanks to Alison and her ridiculous reporting this morning, that's been fixed." While Tamsyn thought Alison had been irresponsible in her newscast and half the shit she said had nothing to do with the headlines, she had to admit, discussing the fact that Carter wasn't her dad helped her and Noir's cause.

"That young woman is lucky I didn't run into her today," Weezer said. "But I don't want to get sidetracked with that. I need to show you something. You might have seen it before in your mother's missing persons file."

"Okay." Tamsyn swallowed.

Weezer reached into her pocket and pulled out a folded piece of paper. "I should have brought this up when we were talking the day of Merlot's wedding. But the conversation never circled back to this."

"What is it?"

"A text your mom sent me an hour before our altercation."

"What does it say?" Tamsyn asked.

"Why don't you read it," Carter said.

Weezer stretched out her arm.

Tamsyn took the paper with a shaky hand. Fred had sworn to her that everything he had was in the files.

But she knew that wasn't true because she'd never seen the note Anna had from her mother that she shared with the Holiday Showcase committee. Fred mentioned he hadn't entered it into evidence because it didn't name anyone. That didn't make sense. Fred was a rules man, and he did everything by the book.

Carter had asked if Tamsyn minded if he sent the note to a forensic friend of his to analyze the handwriting for authenticity. She'd agreed.

She trusted Carter. Of all the people in this town, he'd always proven to be levelheaded, even where his own family was concerned. Though he did some ass-backward things.

She mentioned to Fred that Carter had sent the note to be analyzed. Fred hadn't appreciated that fact. He'd gone as far as to say he wouldn't accept it into evidence and would run his own evaluation of the note.

That wasn't uncommon, but if it had been any other case, Fred wouldn't have been angered by the situation. He would have understood the independent study, done his own, and let good police work stand up in a court of law.

Elizabeth: *I need to talk with you. Can you meet me in town in an hour? We need to clear the air and set things straight. Please. It's important.*

Weezer: *Sure. I have to head in to pick up some things for Carter. I'll meet you in front of Green Bean.*

Tamsyn lifted her gaze. "I've never seen this before. It's not in the file. Fred has never mentioned it."

"That's strange," Weezer said. "I showed him my cell. He took screenshots. Printed it. Thought it would be a good idea to have it with the paperwork."

"My mother's case file isn't very large, so I can't imagine that it got lost, but it's possible that it got misfiled. We all know the former chief of police wasn't the best at his job."

"That brings me to something else that I'm wondering if it ever made it into that file," Carter said. "Were you aware that we received a call from your mom's cell five days after she disappeared?"

"You what?" She stood, sloshing her wine down the front of her shirt. "Why is this the first I'm hearing of that? Carter, you promised me you wouldn't keep things from me. That there would be no more secrets."

"I didn't keep anything from you," Carter said with a deep tone. "Again, I reported that call. Showed the police, which included Fred. But you should know it was a hang-up. There was no one on the other end. And her phone and car were found a day or two later. It turned out to be a dead end. However, I'm struggling with why it wasn't in any of the reports." Carter held up his hand. "Unless Fred was simply trying to protect you, which I understand. I'm just not sure why these were left out or what else isn't in that file."

She eased back into the sofa. "May I keep this?"

"Of course," Weezer said.

"Is there any reason you don't want me telling Fred I know about these two items?" Tamsyn asked.

"I doubt those things will help with anything, but feel free to do whatever you need to with the information." Carter glanced toward the ceiling.

"Is there something else you're not telling me?"

"It's not that," Carter said. "It's just that no matter whose remains those bones turn out to be, if foul play is determined, I'm sure a search warrant is coming to my doorstep."

"Probably sooner than later," Tamsyn agreed.

"I want to get ahead of that and I'd like you to go through every inch of this house. The winery. Every building. Every nook and cranny before that happens."

"That's a little unethical," Tamsyn said.

"It's better than us going through this place and possibly finding something else and then being accused of tampering with it. Or being tempted to hide it." Carter arched a brow. "At least if it was you, I'd know it would be handled properly."

"Are you saying you don't trust my department? Fred? You put him in office." Tamsyn took a large gulp of wine before setting it on the coffee table. She had her own reservations about the Candlewood Falls Police Department. A few things had fallen through the cracks, but that didn't mean they were incompetent. It meant that things weren't put in the right place.

It happened.

Carter exchanged glances with Weezer. "It's not about trust. I have no issue with Fred. But I don't understand why these things weren't told to you. It's something that Fred and I discussed in the past, when you first joined the force and started using your own contacts to conduct a personal search."

"You've got to be kidding me. The two of you talked about that?" she asked. "Did you also sit around discussing who my father might be? That you weren't my dad?"

Carter rubbed the back of his neck. "Those topics did come up, but he's never wanted you to pursue that search and I chose not to tell him I was helping you. I figured that was your business."

"Damn right it was," she mumbled. She let out a long breath. "If I were to conduct any kind of search, it would have to be under the pretense of helping my boyfriend with something. Inventory at the winery. Cleaning out his childhood bedroom. I don't know and I certainly don't like the way this is feeling. But I do get why you'd want me to do it."

"This has less to do with protecting ourselves from what might be coming," Weezer said. "If that were the case, we'd do it ourselves."

"It's more about the feeling that someone is gunning for us. That too many things didn't get filed properly. And the fact that you might not actually be part of any search, but only allowed to be there as a courtesy."

She hadn't thought about that, but Carter was right. "Okay. I'll do it. But if I find anything, we have to call Fred."

"Understood," Carter said.

"The current force is comprised of a lot of young officers, but there are two old-timers left. Jake Harlow and Mark Rose. They spend all their time in administration these days, but do you know what their roles were back in the day?"

"Mark was in your role, basically second-in-command. Jake was a beat cop," Carter said.

"Why didn't you want Mark as chief of police?" She knew at one time Mark was high up the ladder, but for some reason, she always thought Fred had been second to Jack Harper.

Weezer laughed. "Mark's a nice guy, but the first thing Fred did was put him behind a desk. Have you ever wondered why?"

"No," Tamsyn said. "I was twenty when Fred took on the role. I was away at college. When I came back and finally agreed to work for Fred, Mark was already behind a desk and loving it. I didn't think to question it and he's retiring the first of the year."

"It's about time. That man is ten years older than me," Carter said. "That was one reason I didn't want to back him. But the bigger reason was he has no backbone." Carter laughed. "While Fred can't stand up to Anna to save his ass, he can to the rest of this town. I once saw him go head-to-head with Silas. Even I chose my words wisely with that man, and he's one of my best friends since childhood."

"Talk about someone who's changed after falling in love." Growing up, Tamsyn used to think of Silas as the mountain man. A guy who could tame wild animals and probably killed them with his bare hands too.

Carter waggled his finger. "Nope. Silas has always been like that. Claudia just brought it out to the general public."

"Well, he's a lot softer than he used to be and he stopped giving me the stink eye every time I have to remind him he can't park wherever he wants." Tamsyn glanced at her watch. "I hate to cut this short, but I promised Noir I'd cook for him, and that is not my strong suit."

"Well, then I have the solution." Weezer popped to her feet. "I have so much food in my fridge it's insane. There happens to be a full spaghetti pie and a loaf of fresh bread. Take that. He'll never know the difference."

Carter laughed. "Oh, yes, he will, but he'll be happy for the meal. It's his favorite."

Tamsyn groaned. "I know. He's handed me the recipe twice and both times I butchered it."

Weezer laughed. "One of these days, I'll have you over and show you proper."

"You don't know what you're getting into. It's like teaching someone who has two left feet how to dance." In the matter of a week, Tamsyn felt more comfortable in the River home than she had going shopping with Anna her entire time living with her. It should feel strange, or at the very least, a little abnormal.

Except, it felt like home.

10

NOIR

"My mother made this." Noir stuffed his mouth full of pasta. He closed his eyes and savored all the flavors that tickled his taste buds. The sauce had just the right amount of spices with a hint of lemon. That was his mother's secret. And it was so good. He sat back and smiled. "I can't believe you tried to pass this off as yours."

"I did no such thing." Tamsyn raised her glass. "I just didn't correct you when you mentioned how wonderful it smelled when you walked through the door."

He laughed. "You let me believe you slaved for hours over this meal."

She rolled her eyes. "I didn't have it in me to cook. I think I've slept three hours in the last twenty-four."

"Well, as soon as we're done. I'll do the dishes and you can climb into bed."

"I like the sound of that." She took a piece of bread and piled a bite of pasta on top.

"How did things go with my parents?"

"It was interesting," she admitted. "I decided not to tell them about the necklace."

"Why not?"

"In part because they want us to search the grounds." She took a gulp of wine. "And I suppose the same reason I'm not telling Fred. I don't trust anyone completely, and I feel like that necklace is leverage."

"You trust me."

"You have no reason to lie to me," she said. "Except maybe to protect your parents and the rest of your family."

He narrowed his stare. "Are you implying that I would hold something back?"

"If I were in your position, I'd consider it."

Noir wiped his mouth with his napkin and leaned back, contemplating his next words. His parents could be a lot. His mother had meddled in all her children's lives to the point she'd pushed her four oldest right out of the business and her three youngest hadn't even wanted to come work for her when they went off to college.

But the one thing all seven of them could say without a shadow of a doubt was that both of their parents loved them with every fiber of their beings. Everything they did was because they had wanted what was best for their kids. Looking back on his life—and the history of his parents—the only true criminal thing they had done was send Talbot away.

But no one could fault his father for that one. Richard would have killed Talbot and her mother. A fact that was undeniable.

Noir could understand why Tamsyn had some reservations about his mom. But he needed her to have the same about Anna.

He believed that Fred loved and cared for Tamsyn. He'd always been there for her at school functions, showing support. Anna only came when it served a purpose. When it made her look good, not when Tamsyn needed her the most. "Anything my parents have done—even if it wasn't right—they did out of love."

"Not to bring up old pains, but they drove a wedge between Chablis and Dax. It cost them seventeen years."

"You're right. My mom did a number on them. But Dax's mom had a hand in that as well. They all wanted Dax to follow his dreams. If he and Chablis hadn't broken up, he'd never have become an NHL star, and who knows, he could have resented Chablis in the long run, something my sister and her husband have discussed and accepted. They have no regrets."

"Why are we talking about this?"

"Even though my folks didn't come out and tell you everything right out of the gate, that doesn't mean you can't trust them. They are between a rock and a hard place. But their willingness to give you full access should tell you something about who they are."

"We're dancing around something that you want to get off your chest and it's starting to annoy the fuck out of me." She pushed her plate to the side. "Just say it."

"I want you to think about who had access to this cottage and to my parents' house."

"Oh, I get it. You don't think Fred and Anna are trustworthy?"

"Don't put words in my mouth," Noir said. "Fred's a stand-up guy. He's been the chief of police for ten years and his record is impeccable. It's Anna who concerns me and I just told you why."

"Just because she twists things and manipulates things doesn't make her an evil woman." Tamsyn stood, strolling toward the liquor cabinet. She pulled down a bottle of whiskey and poured herself three fingers.

She'd always been more of a whiskey girl than a wine chick. Although, wine had been growing on her, but when conversations got tough, she went for the hard stuff.

Noir wasn't sure if she reached for the beverage because she disagreed or because she was conflicted. The only thing he was sure of was she'd gone into work and defense mode.

That was never a good sign.

"Your mom does the same thing when she gets the chance," Tamsyn said. "I watched that three-legged race. She cheated and all because she needs to be the center of attention, just like Anna."

"My mom didn't win. And Silas cheated too." Noir laughed. "But my mom cheats every year, and everyone lets her because outside of Mrs. Cummings, no one wants to organize the Holiday Showcase and let's face it. My mom puts on a better show."

"Okay. I'll give you that." Tamsyn leaned against the counter in the center of the kitchen. "But Weezer is a manipulator. You've said so yourself, or are you going to have amnesia about the time she forced you into going out for a sport."

He smacked his forehead. "God, no. And that was awful. However, she was worried about how antisocial of a kid I was. She wanted me to make friends outside of my twin. Looking back, it wasn't the worst semester of my life."

"Are you kidding me? God, I wish I saved our texts. You were miserable, especially standing on the sidelines, almost never seeing the field." She shook her head. "That was only made worse when you did play and you either fumbled or ran in the wrong direction."

"Yeah. That was embarrassing. But at least I understand the game now. I actually enjoy watching it with my family on Thanksgiving. It's given me something to bond over with my brothers and dad."

"You never played football again."

"Of course not. I sucked at it. However, I immediately went and joined two clubs at school because of that experience. Both Nebbiolo and I did and we made a couple of friends thanks to my mom's meddling. She might not go about things in the best way, but she's always been able to gauge what's best for us."

Tamsyn laughed. "Oh, really. I think some of your siblings might have a different perspective about how Weezer handled their situations. Like Riesling. That was tough to watch what she and her daughter went through."

"Again, my mom was right about that shitbag ex of my sister." He held up his hand. "I don't agree with how my mother went about some things, especially the way she treated Chablis when Malbec left town. That was downright mean. But everything she does comes out of love. Can you say the same thing about Anna? Or shall I remind you of how she embarrassed the hell out of you when you didn't want to go to the prom and she bought you a dress and bribed the richest, most popular boy in school to take you."

"Christ. That had to be the worst night of my high school life. Hunter Wellington is still a dick." Tamsyn lifted her glass and downed half of it. "But that doesn't make her a bad person."

"I didn't say that either. But we both know Anna is about show. About what other people think. My mother couldn't care less. I get you don't completely trust my mom. In your shoes, I might not either. But my dad? I don't understand that. Which is why I'm not comprehending why you're keeping the information about the necklace to yourself."

"I've trusted Carter ever since I found out he wasn't my father," Tamsyn said. "Without question or reservation. But he'll always stand by his wife. I have no idea how that necklace got into your bathroom. I know neither one of us put it there. Zinny lived here before you did and she would have no reason to do that."

"Neither would my folks and don't say unless one of them forgot."

She arched a brow. "I'm not accusing your parents of anything."

"But you're thinking it."

"Of course I am. I have to. I'm a cop. I have to look at everything."

"Alright," Noir said. "Are you considering Anna could have done that too?"

"So much for never talking about this again," she muttered. She downed the rest of her drink. "There are only three scenarios that make sense. Three culprits. The first being your mother. I'm sorry, but that's where this points. But if not her, then someone is setting her up. That begs who and why. My guess would be whoever my biological father is. If not him, well, someone who hates Weezer and right now, the only person who comes to mind is Anna or Mrs. Cummings, but where's the motive in the last one?" She held up her hand. "If I take out the body found in the vineyard, one could argue that someone is simply fucking with

Weezer, trying to make her look bad so she has to give up the Holiday Showcase. But I don't believe in coincidences. There is no way the items found and the body are not connected, making it harder for me to believe it's because of the stupid showcase. That motivation is too weak. There has to be more to it. However, we won't know until we find out who was buried in that shallow grave."

"What you're saying is that Anna didn't have a motive to hurt your mom, but my mother did." Noir had walked right into that statement, even though that wasn't where he was going. "Only, the rumor isn't true and everyone knows it now."

Tamsyn pinched the bridge of her nose. "It's not the rumor that gives her a motive. It's the accusation and the fight that everyone witnessed that gives her motive."

Noir pressed his hands on the table and stood. He sucked in a deep breath and let it out slowly. "Anna has hated my mother since high school. She has said some pretty nasty things and has even threatened my mother."

"Threat is a strong word," Tamsyn said. "And having a grudge against Weezer for bullshit in high school, or over the stupid Holiday Showcase, doesn't warrant this level of revenge."

"But doesn't it?"

"I've seen a lot of weird shit as a cop and motive is always a key element. Without it, we have no case."

"I feel as though you're making excuses for Anna," Noir said.

"I'm not. I'm looking at every angle, and to be honest, neither Anna nor Weezer make sense to me. But I'm a cop. It's my job. Hell, I have to look at everyone on this winery as a possible suspect. That includes you."

"Sleeping with the enemy." He chuckled, trying to lighten the mood. He didn't want to fight. He didn't even want her to compromise her position. This was about understanding her decision and maybe helping where he could. "If we're talking motive, what would your biological father's motive be?"

"I've thought a lot about that too." She reached for the whiskey, topping off her glass. "If my biological father doesn't want me to find out the truth, he could be redirecting the focus," Tamsyn said.

"That could mean he's been right here the whole time. But why would he do that?"

"Because he's married. Because he's a pillar of this community and has too much to lose. And maybe he has a beef with your mother. That's an angle I need to look at. Or maybe with Carter. Another thing to consider. While just about everyone likes your dad, there are a few criminals who can't stand him, and one potential man on his list of potential fathers for me is Richard Berkin."

"Jesus. That fucking asshole."

Tamsyn nodded.

"He's in prison."

"Maybe so, but he's still got reach and from what I've learned today, he's still got people working for him," Tamsyn said. "Your dad said he wouldn't agree to a paternity test, but Talbot agreed to do one. So, if she's my half-sibling, I'll know my answer."

"That would be fucked up."

"I used to really want to know who my father was. I thought maybe he didn't know about me. I had this idea in my head that if he knew the truth, he'd welcome me with open arms, but now, I'm not so sure."

Noir closed the gap. He took the glass from her hands and set it on the counter before taking her into his arms. "I wish none of this was happening. I'm sorry if I came off like an asshole."

"I get it." She rested her hands on his shoulders. "Especially when it comes to the necklace. I know I should put it in an evidence bag and turn it over. That would be the proper thing to do. But something in my gut is telling me to hold on to it."

He palmed her cheek. "You've always told me that you trust your instincts, even when your training tells you otherwise."

"When Fred finds out, he might fire me. He threatened to do that to me the last time. Only, I was right and he let it go with a warning, reminding me that there are procedures and rules for a reason. That I was lucky the asshole got locked up for fifteen years instead of getting off, which could have happened because of me."

"But as you said, your gut was right."

"Sometimes you really are good for my ego." She rested her head on his shoulder. "I want you to know that I hear you. This whole thing just sucks, and Anna has texted me four times today, telling me all the reasons why I should dump you."

He hugged her close. "I can't believe I'm going to say this considering I all but accused her of planting things, but she could honestly be concerned about your well-being and this is a shitshow. Everyone is talking about one more buried secret at the winery."

"I remember when Trey dug up a coffin full of illegal adoption papers. That could have been the end of this winery."

"That unearthed things that my family is still dealing with," Noir said. "I'm not sure my dad has ever fully come to terms with learning about his father's affair or the fact he had a sibling who died before he had a chance to meet her." He kissed Tamsyn's temple. "Why don't you go crawl into bed. I'll clean up from dinner and then I have some orders I need to go through on my computer. Will it bother you if I do that at the table?"

"I'm sure I'll be out as soon as my head hits the pillow." She patted his chest. "Make sure you wake me up in the morning. I have twenty-four hours off and I want to get started on this project your parents gave us."

"I hope we don't find anything related to your mom, or anything else for that matter. My family has dealt with enough over the years. We're all finally getting along. All working together. It's nice for a change."

"I hope so too." She wiggled out of her jeans, leaving them in the middle of the room. She tossed her sweater on the sofa.

"If we're going to live together, you really need to stop being such a slob." The words tumbled out of his mouth while his heart lurched to the center of his throat. It wasn't as if he hadn't thought about the prospect of having Tamsyn in his life permanently. But that was a shitty way to ask someone to move in. His dad would be so disappointed and his mother would wring his neck.

"Excuse me?" She turned, staring at him in her lacy boy shorts and matching bra that barely kept the girls in. "What did you say?"

He groaned. It was impossible to take his eyes off her when she stood there with her hands firmly planted on her sexy, round hips. "I might have suggested we live together."

"No. You implied I'm messy."

He chuckled. "There's no implication in that. Why do you think we've almost always spent the night at my place? You never pick up after yourself."

"My kitchen is always clean."

He shouldn't laugh, but it was impossible not to. "Because you don't cook and when you do, I need to come over and sterilize."

"You're just being mean now."

"And you're avoiding my proposition."

"Moving in here would really piss off Anna and certainly give this town more to gossip about." She turned and pulled back the covers. "But my landlord wants to raise my rates. What would our rent be?"

"You've got to be joking? My parents don't make me pay for this place. And they won't be charging you rent either. Not if you're living here with me."

"I guess I'm moving in." She tossed her bra in his direction. "I think the dishes can wait until morning."

"You know how much I hate letting food dry on the plates."

She dangled her panties on her index finger.

"They can wait." He ripped off his shirt, raced across the room, and dove into bed, laughing. He took her into his arms and kissed her hard. His heart filled with more love than he'd ever experienced before.

Even though there was so much chaos that swarmed around them like bees, he knew without doubt, Tamsyn was the person he was meant to love.

11

TAMSYN

Tamsyn pulled down a box from the closet in what used to be Noir and Nebbiolo's bedroom. Carefully, she dumped the contents on the mattress. It had been filled with memorabilia from Noir's days at Candlewood Falls High School.

"I was told you were in here." Zinny came barreling into the room. "Mind if I hide out here with you for a bit?"

"Not at all, but what are we hiding from?"

"Taking a break from my baby." Zinny dropped onto the corner of the bed and sighed. "Don't get me wrong. I love being a mom and Crystal is such a good baby most days, but my teenage son is easier to deal with than the reincarnation of me, Reisling, Ashling, and my mother."

"Do you have any idea how weird it is to hear you say *teenage son*?"

"I am adopting him." Zinny lifted a notebook. "Serena has signed the papers. It's all but a done deal. We just need the courts to sign off on it."

"I never really knew Serena. Or Toby growing up. I understand Serena's in prison for a few years, but I struggle with why any woman would give up parental rights when she's going to get out."

"To be totally transparent, we didn't think she'd agree to it. But her father talked her into it by telling her the only way he'd help her financially when she got out was if she did the right thing and let TJ have a normal life. He's happy with Toby and me and he's thriving at CWF Prep. Having Serena back in his life would only cause that poor boy more pain. I wish I believed deep down Serena believed that, but all she cares about is money." Zinny flipped open the notebook.

"Are you sure about that?"

"Oh yeah. Her father told Toby she asked what kind of support he offered. As in, what kind of car he'd give her, the amount of monthly allowance, and if he would make her have a job."

"Shit. That's cold."

"Tell me about it." Zinny swiped at her cheeks.

"TJ is damn lucky to have you and Toby for loving parents."

"Thank you. I appreciate the kind words." Zinny ran her fingers across the pages. "Oh my God. This is hysterical. You've got to see this."

"What?" Tamsyn set aside the yearbook she'd been thumbing through. She wasn't sure why she'd opened it, except to see what kinds of messages her classmates wrote to Noir. She never had hers signed. She didn't have that many friends and she figured she'd be too depressed ten years later when she opened that fucker up.

Noir must have felt the same way because she hadn't seen a single signature.

Zinny held up the notebook, showing off the inside cover. The words *Noir and Tamsyn* with a heart traced around stared back at her like a rocket. "I knew my brother had a crush on you, but I didn't expect him to be such a girl about it."

"I didn't know." She took the pad from Zinny and ran her fingers over the letters. She flipped the page. "This is a journal." She lifted her gaze. "I shouldn't be reading this."

"Then I will." Zinny snatched it, jumping to her feet.

"Come on. We shouldn't."

"Oh, we absolutely should." Zinny sat on the windowsill. There was no arguing with her when she got like this.

And if Tamsyn was being honest, she wanted to know what Noir might have been thinking back in the day.

"It's dated, and this would have been his senior year," Zinny said. *"My father always says writing thoughts down is helpful. I've been doing this now for a year, and I can't say that it's doing anything but letting me bare my soul. But I can't really tell anyone. Nebbiolo, who I tell everything to, wouldn't understand. He'd poke fun at me and this isn't a laughing matter.*

The person I want to tell, well, that would be a disaster for more than one reason. For so long, Tamsyn and I have kept our friendship private." Zinny lifted her gaze. "What the hell does that mean?"

"You know Noir was always kind to me." Tamsyn took a folder and opened it. Tucked inside were all his report cards. "We did text more than we let on, but with the way the other kids treated us because of the rumors, we kept our distance while at school."

"You learn something new every day." Zinny adjusted the notebook. *"From the beginning, we both agreed it was for the best. My father has said the rumors aren't true. So has my mother. I believe them. So does Tamsyn. It's utterly absurd. I want to act on my feelings, but doing that, I not only risk more ridicule, but I could lose my best friend and the one person who means as much to me as my family.*

And now she's going to prom with fucking Hunter.

I should be taking her. I want to. But holy shit, that would cause a stir bigger than my mother walking down Main Street in curlers holding a loaded shotgun.

If only there was a way to make the rumor mill go away so I could tell Tamsyn that I love her."

"What the fuck are you doing, Zinny?" Noir flew into the room and snatched the notebook from her hands. "Where did you get this?" He snapped it shut, tucking it under his arm.

"And you." He pointed to Tamsyn. "I can't believe you sat there and let her read that shit."

Tamsyn covered her mouth to hide her smile. Part of her felt bad she had invaded his personal space. Those were his private thoughts from when he'd been a teenager. However, his words had not only been unexpected, mind-blowing, and insanely sweet, but they touched a part of her heart that had always been reserved for him.

She might not have written her thoughts in a notebook. She might not have even realized how deep her feelings were for Noir back in high school. But he'd been her ride or die for as long as she could remember.

Even when they dated other people.

"I'm so glad you find this amusing," he mumbled. "I thought Mom got rid of this stuff when I moved out."

"You should have seen the stuff I found in my old room." Zinny stood. "Toby had a field day with some of those things, especially my *who should I marry* binder that I put together when I was twelve."

"Oh, sweet Jesus. Who was in that?" Tamsyn asked.

Zinny tapped her temple and glanced toward the ceiling. "Officer Bob. Dax. Sam Wilde. The Zamboni guy at CWF Prep when Dax played there."

"Let me put it this way," Noir said. "Any man who was ten years older and had a pulse. Including her husband."

"Yeah, I did have a crush on him." Zinny smiled. "Speaking of the love of my life. I better go give him a hand with the little munchkin."

"We appreciate him taking the day off work to help with this search." Noir sat on the bed, tossing the notebook into a box. "He's in the den with Dad."

"Toodles." Zinny blew a kiss and scurried out of the room.

"I should have destroyed those notebooks." Noir sorted through a few of the items, which included a few photos. She leaned over his shoulder. "You look so young."

"I was such a dorky kid."

"I thought you were handsome." She palmed his cheek.

"You're just saying that because of what my little sister read." He smacked his forehead. "So embarrassing."

"You really thought you were in love with me back in high school?"

He laughed. "I've been in love with you since forever. It's not that part I'm embarrassed about. It's that I even kept a stupid journal. Put that on paper. It's weird."

"No, it's not. It's one way to deal with thoughts and feelings. I never could because Anna would have read it and used it against me. You're lucky you felt the freedom to have something like that, especially in such a large family."

"Well, I'm sure my mom has read it, since it's still in this house." He took her hand and kissed it. "Which would explain so much of why she's been acting the way she has about our relationship. As if she and my dad have been expecting it to happen."

"At least she didn't say anything about it. That would have been truly embarrassing," Tamsyn said. "What else did you write in that thing?"

"It's mostly all about you. A few random things about stuff that happened with my family. I stopped doing it when you told me you were in love with Billy Johnson. My thoughts turned pretty dark and I didn't want those to be in black and white."

"Ugh. That's a relationship I'd like to forget."

"You lost your virginity to him." Noir arched a brow and puckered his lips like he'd just swallowed an entire lemon. "Something I wish I never knew."

"Oh, and who you slept with for the first time is a better choice? Little Miss Sunshine herself. I fucking hated Lori Samuels. To me, that felt like a slap in the face. You paraded her around town on your arm like you won the lottery."

"I most certainly did not. Sadly, I was using her to get back at you for Billy. It was my dad who actually pointed out that fact to me."

"Really? That's a little shocking."

"Oddly, my folks have been right about each and every single one of their children and who they belong with."

"What about Zinny and Toby? Did they see that one coming? Because he's like sixteen years older than her." Tamsyn collected the items and tucked them back in the box. There was nothing that didn't belong in this room. So far, there hadn't been anything in the house that was out of place.

"Not like you're thinking. But when the shit went down with Chablis' medical records and Toby hired my dad to represent him, they saw the way Toby looked at my little sister. They couldn't deny it if they tried, and they didn't do anything to stop it," Noir said. "Nebbiolo is the only one who has thrown them for a loop, but June is perfect for him and my parents see that."

"She is sweet." She leaned in, brushing her lips across Noir's mouth. "And so are you. I love you. I did have feelings for you back in high school. But the rumors, and where my head was at, I couldn't have ever acted on them."

"I know. I doubt we were mature enough to handle the backlash anyway." He lifted the box and shoved it into the closet.

Tamsyn's cell buzzed in her back pocket. She pulled it out and stared at the screen. "Holy shit."

"What's wrong?"

"It's a text from Fred." She glanced up, catching Noir's gaze. "I need to go into the station."

"Why?"

"The report on the remains is back." She swallowed. "I don't think he'd want me to come in if it wasn't my mother."

"You don't know that." He grabbed her hand. "But either way, I'm coming with you."

She wasn't going to argue. She could use the support of someone who loved her no matter what.

Tamsyn

Holding Noir's hand, ignoring the stares from her co-workers, Tamsyn made her way through the bullpen. Normally, the station had always been her home away from home. It represented safety. A place where she could collect her thoughts. Be herself. Be free of judgment. Even when gossip reared its ugly head, this space became a cocoon of protection, wrapping her in a bubble. No one here whispered behind her back or treated her like she didn't belong. If they thought it, they didn't show it.

She turned the corner into Fred's office. The heavy beat of her heart thumped against her chest.

"Tamsyn," Fred said. "I'm sorry, but Noir needs to step into the lobby."

"Is this official business? Or personal?" Tamsyn asked.

"It's a gray area." Fred stood, looping his fingers through his belt loop.

Power move.

Fuck.

That said it all.

"Gray area or not, unless this is about my job specifically—a case I'm working, an issue in this department—he's staying, because if this is about what I think it is, I have a right to have my boyfriend with me for moral support."

Fred pressed his hands on the desk and leaned forward. "I know I don't have to tell you why he shouldn't be here." He narrowed his stare and furrowed his brow. "And you have me for support."

Shit. She'd gone and hurt Fred's feelings. That, she hadn't wanted to do. Even though Fred wasn't her father, she did care. He'd been a good role model. He'd supported her and did his best to be there. He wasn't a bad man. But right now, she needed Noir more and Fred to understand that. "I'm sorry, Fred. I want Noir here with me while you actually say the words. Besides, when we're done, you'll have to get in a car and drive to his parents' house and tell them anyway. Might as well kill two birds with one stone."

"Have it your way, but Noir, you need to give me your cell." Fred held out his hand.

"Why do I need to do that, sir?" Noir asked.

"Because I can't have you calling your parents or

anyone else in your family until I've had the chance to chat with your folks." Fred wiggled his fingers.

Noir pulled his phone from his pocket and placed it in Fred's palm.

"Thank you, son. Now, one of you please close the door and take a seat." Fred gripped the armrests of his big leather chair. He rolled it around to the side of the desk, closer to her, and eased himself into it. Taking her by the hands, he let out an audible sigh.

Noir tenderly, lovingly rubbed the back of her neck.

She swallowed as memories pummeled her brain. They were rapid-fire, coming at her from all directions. She could barely catch glimpses of each one. Her mind searched her past like a computer going through massive amounts of code, searching for the missing link.

It landed on the day she came home from school and waited—as she always did—for her mom to come home from work. Her mother had been working in housekeeping for a small hotel in the next town. It had been the longest she'd ever held a job. Later, Tamsyn had learned that Carter had helped her get that job.

But that night, her mother never came home. Tamsyn waited until midnight to call the police.

Fred had been the officer to show up. There was nothing he could do until her mom had been missing for twenty-four hours. However, he did make inquiries before that time had elapsed. He also brought a young and scared Tamsyn back to his place for the night.

And that's where she stayed ever since.

Fred had been kind. Gentle. He respected Tamsyn's feelings. He never treated her like a child. He'd been upfront and honest, something she respected.

"I'm sorry, Tamsyn. The remains were indeed your mother's." Fred squeezed her hands.

Noir didn't say anything. He didn't have to. His presence and sweet touch were enough.

"Foul play?" She couldn't think past being a cop. The crushing pain that grew from the center of her chest and radiated through her body couldn't seep into the real world. She couldn't let it out. It was as if it ignited and then froze.

"That's going to take a couple more days," Fred said.

"Who's heading up the investigation?" Her eyes burned, but no tears appeared. Deep down, she'd known her mother had been dead for years. She didn't need instincts to tell her that. There had been no reason for her mother to disappear. If had been a few years before, she might have believed it. Only, she still would have concluded her mother had died. But perhaps of different causes.

"State is taking over the forensics and we've put together a task force. I've named Eddy as lead from our department and put together a team with two detectives from State and two from us. You will not be part of it." Fred ran his hand up and down her arm. It should feel comforting. Loving. But all she felt was a vast emptiness the size of the Grand Canyon. His gesture voided out years of hoping but knowing the truth at her core.

A quiet anger crawled across her skin.

"You'll be allowed to be present. We will inform you directly as will State regarding the forensics. But you will not interfere, insert yourself, or be part of anything we do." He inched closer. "Can I get you some water?" He tilted his head. "I'm a little worried about you."

"I'm fine," she said. "That grave was shallow. I saw it. It was fresh. She'd been moved. What do we know about that?" Tamsyn wasn't sure if she was asking for herself or for Noir.

He still hadn't said a single word, and she loved him even more for that. He knew what she needed and when. He was there to be a beating heart and he did it well.

"We're not having that conversation right now." Fred lowered his chin. "I want you to take a couple of weeks off."

"No," she said. "I'll go crazy. I need to work and I'm gonna want access."

"I told you that you can be present in anything related to your mom's case," Fred said. "You need to take time for yourself."

"Fred's right." Noir's hot breath rolled across her body like a warm blanket.

Only, she wanted to rip it off and toss it back.

This was the last thing she needed. If she wasn't

working, she wasn't close to the case and Noir should understand that.

"And if you need something to do, we can always use a hand at the winery." Noir kissed her temple.

Well, shit. She hadn't thought about that.

"If I take time off, you're not going to shut me down? I can come in here and look at my mother's files? I can go with Eddy when he's interviewing someone or checking on a lead?"

"Yes," Fred said. "Unless there's a really huge conflict." Fred shifted his gaze. "No offense, young man, but if you ever need to be interviewed, Tamsyn won't be there."

"None taken, sir," Noir said.

"Okay. I'll take the time. But I want to see the forensics report that State sent." An intense jab to her gut hit like a ton of bricks.

Her mother was dead.

Really dead.

She'd been moved to a shallow grave. Her bones tossed in there like yesterday's trash.

Why?

Who would do that?

Tamsyn's eyes watered. No. She wouldn't cry. Not in this office. She sucked in a deep breath, reining in her emotions.

"You can read it in the car while we drive over to the winery," Fred said. "Tamsyn, you ride with me.

Noir, you follow. You'll get your phone after we get there."

She stood. "Let's roll."

Tamsyn didn't want many things in life. She wanted what most people did.

A career she enjoyed.

A man to love.

She had those things. She valued them. Appreciated them. They made her happy.

But not whole.

The only thing that would do that would be finding out who her biological father was and putting away whoever did this to her mother.

She wouldn't rest until those two things completed her puzzle of life.

12

CARTER

Carter leaned back and stared at the smoke billowing from the end of the cigar. It had been years since he'd picked one up. Over a decade.

Weezer was going to kill him.

Right after she made him get undressed, outside, and then take a shower before entering *her* house. Of course, he'd still have to sleep in one of the other six bedrooms.

Six fucking bedrooms.

He loved that damn house. Raised his family in it. But they were all grown and gone.

Malbec and Eliza Jane had built a beautiful home on the winery over the ridge. It overlooked the vineyards on the north end of the property. Carter saw their kids almost every day and loved every second of it.

Chablis and Dax lived on the outskirts of town

about ten miles away with their two kids. He saw them almost as much.

Reisling and Trey and their brood lived ten miles in the other direction in a massive house they built. Trey was a good man and took great care of his girl. He was a fine doctor, and Carter would forever be in the man's debt for saving his life.

Merlot and Talbot had found each other again. Reuniting them had brought Carter more happiness than he could have ever imagined. Finding out about Corbin had been an unexpected joy. They had settled in nicely in a house outside of town. Their family was about to get a little bit bigger.

Zinny and Toby, after great deliberation, moved into Carter's family home. Keeping that house in the family warmed his heart. It was meant for love, life, and laughter. His daughter, her husband, and their kids, needed a home like that and he was thrilled to give it to them.

Nebbiolo had shocked the family by running off and marrying his dog trainer. But who he'd married hadn't come as a surprise at all. The second Carter and Weezer saw them together, they knew without a shadow of a doubt that Nebbiolo had found his soulmate. June owned her own home, where they planned on settling and starting a family.

Carter figured that June was already pregnant.

Hence the quick wedding.

Whatever it took for his kids to find happiness. He didn't care. June was the one.

Noir had Tamsyn. Finally. Carter had been watching that love bloom for years. Every girl Noir dated was just someone he passed time with until Tamsyn came around. Carter felt bad for the other women, but this was one situation where even Weezer didn't dare interfere.

Too much history.

Too much pain.

And now they were living in the tiny cottage, which was really a studio. It had been built by his wife's grandfather for nonfamily member employees who needed a place to crash.

It was too small for a couple to stay long term. Malbec and Eliza Jane learned that real quick.

The main house had a pulse, but it was weakening. It needed more than he and Weezer could offer it anymore. It needed a family. It needed youth again.

It was time to pass the torch and there was only one child left.

"What are you doing out here in the cold, old man?" Silas stepped in front of the fire.

Carter puffed on the cigar, making a big smoke ring. He watched it float toward the star-filled sky until it broke apart in the cold winter night.

"Weezer's going to serve your head on a platter for supper," Silas said.

"After the day we had, maybe she'll forgive me."

"Right after she shoots you in the foot with a BB gun."

Carter chuckled. "She never meant to do that. It was an accident."

"Doubtful. You were flirting with another girl. One she didn't like. Your wife is a jealous woman and she shot you on purpose."

"It wasn't me she was aiming for." Carter leaned back in the Adirondack chair, tugging his coat tight. Everyone complained about the cold. In all his years in New Jersey, it never bothered him. He enjoyed the changing of the seasons. He liked the snow in the vineyard. And then watching the grapes blossom in the spring. "I was the dumbass who tried to stop her from hitting Mary Sue in the ass. And for the record, I wasn't flirting with her. She was hitting on me."

"Everyone was always hitting on you." Silas set a glass on the armrest filled with the good stuff on the rocks.

"Thanks. I was contemplating going and getting a refill, but then I would have had to put this out and go inside; it would have been a whole thing."

"My pleasure." Silas eased into a chair and sipped his drink. "Up until that night, we called Weezer by her real name, Shirley."

Carter burst out laughing. "That night changed my life."

"It always amazed me how quickly that nickname stuck. I asked Cordy many times how she managed that. And why that name, of all things, to describe what a woman sounds like during—"

"If you say it, I'll punch you." Carter shook his head. That name was more his fault than Cordy's. Or Weezer's for that matter. "My wife's noises are none of anyone's business but mine and there's no wheezing. Trust me. However, out of shock and utter embarrassment at our predicament, my wife might have hurled a few superlatives at Cordy. I covered her mouth, and it got muffled."

"I still don't understand how Cordy got it to stick overnight."

"She didn't. I did," Carter said. "Cordy might have been the first one to call her Weezer. But I'm the one who adopted it. But it started out as a pet name. Cordy overhead me say it the next morning. I never heard that old bird laugh so hard. Weezer opened her mouth to do what she does best and I covered it again. Cordy called her *The Weezer* in front of a dozen people. When I called her that again later, it just took on a life of its own."

"Well, the name does fit her better than the one her parents gave her." Silas lifted his feet, resting them on a log. "How old were you?"

"Nineteen," Carter said. "I was home for a long weekend. I thought for sure Weezer's old man was going to kill me when he found out what happened. But instead, he handed us the keys to the kingdom and told me if I ever hurt his little girl, he'd castrate me." Carter shifted. He believed that man's statement. "I've loved Weezer for as long as I can remember. My life would be shit without her."

"And boring as fuck."

"Cheers to that." Carter raised his glass and clanked it against Silas'. "I'm sure you've heard by now that the remains found on my property were indeed Elizabeth's."

"Poor Tamsyn. But at least she knows."

"Yeah, but we don't know what happened, when it happened, or how in the hell her body landed in the vineyard." Carter took another long drag of the cigar. Damn, it felt good. Like an old friend he hadn't seen in years. He'd put up with a lot of crazy shit over the years from his wife. Meddling in their children's lives. A secret that drove them to an unwanted divorce and separate homes. It didn't matter that they still had three more children after that and were still very much in love and a couple. It put a strain on them and could have destroyed them.

Weezer could handle one fucking cigar.

"The way Fred and little Eddy acted today, I'm expecting a search warrant by the beginning of the week."

"Why? You said it was obvious the body had been moved and you gave them permission already to search the vineyards."

Carter took a long slow sip of his bourbon. It burned going down. "I suspect that the autopsy will show that Elizabeth was murdered and Fred knows that. There's also some suspect evidence we've already turned over that we found in the china cabinet that belonged to Elizabeth."

"Jesus." Silas tossed his head back and downed half his drink. "I don't begin to understand law or how this shit works, but why on earth would you or Weezer move her body if you killed her? I do know motive matters."

"That's the piece that they will have a hard time with. But there's enough circumstantial evidence, both past and present, to get a judge to sign a warrant and haul our asses to the station as persons of interest."

"How's Noir and Tamsyn taking all this?"

"Noir's as solid as a rock. He's there for his girl, supporting her the best way he knows how." Carter turned his head. "I'm damn proud of that boy. He's managing to straddle being a kind, loving boyfriend and doing what he can to protect this family. Those twins of mine have been lost for as long as I can remember. They didn't take to being bastard children like Zinny did." Carter chuckled. "That daughter of mine wore it like fucking badge of honor."

"She's a chip off the old Weezer," Silas said.

Carter watched the flames snake toward the sky. The logs snapped and crackled, popping little pieces that burned out before they got too far. "I'm worried about Tamsyn, though. It's like she's ten all over again. Emotionless. I can see the pain struggling to break free deep in her eyes. But she's not letting it out. She was like that for years, wandering the town, putting on a fake smile, pretending to be okay while she searched for answers."

"Then she blew up at Weezer," Silas said.

"That girl needed to unleash her emotions somewhere. It hurt Weezer. No doubt about that. But that's water under the bridge. Right now, Tamsyn needs to know she's always got a safe space with us and when she's ready to break down, we'll be there to catch her. But that's kind of an oxymoron now, isn't it?"

"What about Anna and Fred? They raised her. No offense, but they should be that safety net."

Carter closed his eyes. It had always caused him a great deal of pain to see the disconnect between those three. He'd hoped it would be a good fit, but he had his reservations. Mostly about Anna. She wasn't the maternal type. There were people who thought that about Weezer, but they didn't know her, the real woman behind the tough exterior that she'd developed in order to survive a nightmare handed down from generation to generation.

One that she ended.

"Fred's a good man. But he has a job to do. It's going to be tough to compartmentalize between being a parent—and I use that term loosely—and the chief of police."

"Do you regret not taking her in?" Silas had never once asked him that question and it came as a bit of a shock that he chose to do so now.

"Weezer and I couldn't have. Not because of the rumors and not because we were living in separate homes at the time. It wouldn't have been the right environment for Tamsyn at the time. But I've never believed that Fred and Anna's home was either."

"Why do you say that? Is it because you don't like Anna?"

Carter chuckled. "No. But it always struck me as odd why Fred and Anna did that. Fred is inherently good. He does a lot of decent and kind things for the people of this community. But he doesn't go out of his way to do them."

"And his wife only does them if people can see it and tell her what a wonderful person she is. She doesn't do it out of the kindness of her heart; she does it for the attention."

"Bingo." Carter waved his finger. "We can all sit around and joke about Weezer cheating to get the Holiday Showcase. But no one stops her. Why? Because they want her to do it. Granted, my wife likes the attention, but she doesn't do it for that. She does it because she's good at it, and it's one way to give back to the community. When she held the first meeting after the fire, Anna and Mrs. Cummings came in hot. Like scalding hot. They were all fired up and worried that Weezer was going to change everything."

"But she didn't. According to Claudia, she kept everything exactly the same, right down to the lineup of acts, the music, even the decorating ideas."

"Because they were perfect and Weezer's no fool. Why reinvent the wheel."

"Claudia also told me that it was Anna who started making suggestions for changes once the meeting got under way, acting as if the ideas were Weezer's, and not Claudia's."

"That was truly the funny part of the entire meeting," Carter said. "Anna doesn't know how to read a room, much less empathize with a young girl and all the questions that must have been swirling around in Tamsyn's head when her mother went missing. That girl has always been reserved. Even as a toddler. She had to be because of her life circumstances. But she never came out of her shell until she moved out of Anna and Fred's home."

"For a man who doesn't make assumptions, you're making a lot of them about three people's interpersonal relationships."

"I'm commenting on what I've seen over almost thirty years," Carter said.

"Okay. I'll bite. Why do you think that is?"

"Tamsyn doesn't trust easily. She never has. And with good reason. I don't believe she's ever truly trusted Anna with her emotions."

"What about Fred?" Silas asked.

"Oh, she trusts him with a lot more than Anna. She values and respects him, or she wouldn't have taken that job. But I saw the distance between them when Fred came to the house."

"That could have been because Fred was questioning her boyfriend's parents."

Carter shook his head. "She had a few questions of her own for us when Fred left, and they were pretty tough ones too. That girl doesn't hold any punches. No. The distance had nothing to do with her relationship with Noir. It goes deeper and it damn near broke my heart."

"I've told you this a million times over the years, old man, you can't save the world and you need to stop trying."

Carter leaned over and butted out the cigar. "Not the world. Just my family and Noir loves Tamsyn. That makes her family." He took his drink and stood. "We should get back inside. I want to take more of your money before I head home and face my wife about my cigar smoking. It might take the sting out of that lecture."

Noir

"Hey, you." Noir handed Tamsyn a mug of hot chocolate. "What are you doing out here, alone in the dark? I was worried about you." He glanced around the vineyard. The crime scene tape was still draped across the fence and around a few vines, closing off the area.

He wasn't surprised that Tamsyn had wandered out here, only sad that she'd chosen to do it without him.

"I don't know." She gripped the cup and stared at the empty grave. It had been only a foot deep. "I had just meant to sit on the front stoop and get some fresh air."

"It's freezing out here." He wrapped his arm around her, tugging her close, grateful she didn't push him away.

She'd been distant for hours and he couldn't stand the ache that it left in his soul.

"I can barely feel anything," she said. "It's like I'm not even here. Like none of this is real." She turned. "I don't understand Fred. The way he's treating your parents. There isn't enough evidence of anything to be so combative. There's proof the body hadn't been here long. I know that because I read the report."

"I'm not sure you should be telling me that."

"Probably not, but I won't lose my job over it." She rested her head on his shoulder. "The only issue is what your parents found in their china cabinet and the necklace. But no one knows about that. I feel like I'm missing something. My gut tells me that Fred is keeping something from me."

"Why would he do that?"

"To protect me, I guess. But even that doesn't feel right. I'm not a little girl anymore. I'm a grown woman. And a cop." She sniffled. "My mother's dead. Deep down, I accepted that a long time ago. There isn't anything I can do to bring her back. All I can do is find answers. But how am I supposed to do that when one of the people I've believed my whole life was helping me do just that is possibly standing in my way?"

"I'll agree that Fred came in a little hot. But so did you," Noir said.

"Only because I wanted to make sure your folks weren't keeping anything from me because of Fred. I believe what your parents told me. I'm struggling to trust that Fred doesn't already have one of them pegged as guilty, and that's not like him and I want to know why."

"There's no way of shutting off that brain of yours, is there?"

"I wish there was."

"Let's head back to the cottage." Noir kissed her temple. "What did Fred say to you on the way to my parents'?"

She scoffed. "He doesn't believe now is a good time for me to be moving in with you. He wanted me to put the brakes on the relationship, just until the investigation was over."

"While I don't agree, my dad mentioned his own concern about that."

"Why?"

Noir hit the light on his cell, illuminating a pathway through the darkness. "He doesn't want any undue pressure on you. If you feel safe and secure here, then he wants you here. But if you feel conflicted staying on the property, or if you're going to wander to the grave site constantly, then he thought maybe I should go back with you to your place for the time being. Or maybe Dax and Chablis'. They have a garage apartment."

"So, he doesn't think we should call it quits?"

"Neither does my mother," Noir said. "But they understand the situation. It's complicated. They don't want to put you in a difficult position."

"This sucks and taking time off works feels like I'm being sidelined. I can't sit around and do nothing."

"You're not and I'm going to help you. Nebbiolo agreed to cut his honeymoon short. He's coming back tomorrow."

"That's nice of him."

Noir chuckled. "June's got bad morning sickness, so it's for the best anyway."

Tamsyn paused ten paces from the cottage. "She's pregnant?"

"Why do think they ran off and got married? I guess her parents aren't as understanding about those kinds of things as my parents are."

"We're not living in the dark ages. People have kids all the time without being married. That's ridiculous." She marched toward the cottage, pausing at the front door. "Someone left a package." She lifted a manila envelope. "For me."

"That's strange. I was only gone for a half hour." He scanned the area. "There's a fresh set of tire tracks. My dad's at poker and my mom always waits up for him. I'll call her and see if she saw the car that came down."

"Aren't you the little detective." She waved her hand. "Let's see what this is first."

"You're the boss."

"Don't you ever forget it."

Noir helped her with her coat, hanging it up on the rack before shedding his own. He refreshed their cocoa and sat at the island, waiting patiently as she examined the envelope.

"It just has my name on it. Typed. Nothing to indicate where or who it came from." Barely touching it, she lifted the metal prongs and dumped out the pages inside. "It's copies of canceled checks. From your father to my mother."

"That's it?"

"No. There's a sticky note that reads: *hush money*."

"That's bullshit. My dad gave your mom money. He's never denied it." Noir tapped his cell. His mom picked up on the second ring.

"Hello, son. What can I do for you this evening?"

"Did you see a car come down to the cottage in the last half hour or so?"

"I was soaking in the tub, so no. I'm sorry, I didn't. Why, is something wrong?"

"I'm not sure. When do you expect Dad home?"

"Depends on if he's winning or losing," his mom said. "But I suspect within the next hour. Should I have him call you?"

"I'll text him. Thanks, Ma. And lock the doors, okay?"

"I will. Love you, Noir."

"Love you too, Mom." He shot off a quick text to his father.

His dad responded immediately.

Dad: *I have copies of every single check and what it was meant for. I can swing by tonight, or we can go over it all in the morning.*

Noir: *Morning will be fine.*

Dad: *The showcase is in two days. We'll be up early. You text me when you're ready.*

Noir showed Tamsyn the message string.

"Of course your dad has a record of everything." She pushed the papers across the counter. "I'm tired. I don't want to think about this anymore."

"Let's get you to bed."

"I'm not in the mood for that either."

He raised his hands. "I meant so you can sleep. I'm not expecting anything. We live together now. We don't have to have sex every night. I'm not that big of a horndog."

"Oh yes, you are, and if you tried, I'd cave and I just don't want to do that." For the first time in a long while, tears dribbled down her cheeks. They came hard and fast. She covered her mouth. "No. I don't want to do this either."

"But you need to." He lifted her off the stool and carried her to bed. Hugging her close, he let her purge the emotions from her body.

And they weren't silent.

They were guttural.

They tore at his soul and broke his heart.

13

TAMSYN

Tamsyn wrapped her arms around Noir, snuggling in as close as possible, tucking her legs in behind his, enjoying the way their bodies fit.

Last night he hadn't said anything. He held her in his strong, loving arms and let her expunge all the pain she'd been holding in for twenty years.

Crying wasn't something she did. Being a master of her emotions was something she prided herself on. She'd learned at a very young age not to show them. She didn't want her mother to worry. She didn't want anyone to know how scared she was every single day of her life.

After her mother disappeared, it became a necessity to survive in this town. The constant ridicule. The stares. The snickers. The mean remarks from children and grown-ups alike.

And it didn't stop with the townspeople.

She had to endure it occasionally in the place she called home.

Whether Fred and Anna wanted to admit it, or even realized what they were doing, they too said things about her mother they shouldn't have. Or said them when they didn't think she was listening.

Things like how her mother wasn't fit to be a parent.

That she never loved Tamsyn enough, or she would have given her up when she'd been born.

It was mostly Anna, but Fred never stopped her or defended Elizabeth.

Tamsyn ran her hand up and down his biceps, kissing his neck.

"Good morning." He stretched, rolling to face her. He kissed her nose. "What time is it?"

"Seven thirty."

"That means we have plenty of time for my favorite morning activity."

"Are you ever not horny?" She reached inside his underwear, curling her fingers around his length.

His eyes widened. "I think you're the one who woke up with ideas, not me."

"This says otherwise." She stroked gently, but firmly, teasing just the way he liked.

"That's there every morning. It's both a blessing and curse." He lifted her shirt over her head and tossed it across the room. "Just so we're clear. You started this. Not me. But I'm not complaining."

"You've got me on a technicality."

His lips landed on her mouth like a missile seeking its target. He grappled with the rest of her clothing. His hands roamed her body, giving her pleasure in all the right places. Making love to him had been effortless. The first time with any man usually had a hint of awkwardness, but never with him. She'd never been shy in the bedroom, but she didn't come out like gangbusters right out of the gate.

That all changed the moment she climbed into bed with Noir.

She'd fantasized about what it would like to be with him and worried for about two seconds her dreams wouldn't live up to the images in her brain. She'd been pleasantly surprised.

And things had only gotten better.

Noir was like a fine wine.

She rolled him to his back, kissing her way across his chest, down his stomach, greedily taking him into her mouth.

He pooled her hair on the top of her head, threading his fingers through the strands. He was an attentive lover. Kind and gentle. But wild and intense at the same time. She could no longer ever imagine being with anyone else. He was it.

The one.

And she knew it with every fiber of her being.

"Up here," he whispered, tugging gently.

She wiped her lips and smiled.

"You're the devil." He flipped her on her back, pushing her legs apart. He toyed with her nipples, twisting and turning until she begged for more.

He didn't disappoint.

His mouth was like the warm sun and his tongue like the waves lapping against the shore. It was magical and she couldn't take it a second longer.

"I need you, now," she said.

He entered her in a quick thrust. He repeated the motion, over and over again until she cried out his name.

She could barely fill her lungs as he collapsed on top of her, breathless.

Whether sex was a marathon or it was down and dirty fast, it was always the best she ever had.

Running her nails up and down his spine, she allowed herself to forget all the reasons she shouldn't be enjoying this moment.

He rolled to the side, pulling the covers over their bodies. "Best way to start the day."

"You're impossible." She laughed. But she also agreed. She propped herself up on his chest. "I'm sorry about last night."

"Nothing to apologize for." He tucked her hair behind her ears. "You needed to get it out. I'm just glad it didn't happen while you were alone."

"Thank you for being so understanding."

"I love you, Tamsyn. The good, the bad, the tears. All of it. Whatever you need. I'm here for you."

Knock. Knock.

She jumped, clutching the sheets to her chest. "I thought we were meeting your parents at the main house."

"We are." Noir tossed back the covers, found his sweats, and hiked them up over his hips. "They would never come here without calling first. Not unless it was a true emergency, and then they would be pounding on the door, calling my name, begging me to let them in."

"Then who the hell is out there?"

"We're about to find out." He turned.

"No. Wait. Let me at least put some clothes on." She scrambled to find something to put on her body. "This is why you should let me be a slob." Covering herself with a pillow, she raced to the small dresser. She yanked open a drawer and found an oversized sweatshirt and a pair of yoga slacks. Quickly, she dressed.

Knock. Knock.

"I'll be right there," Noir called. "Are you ready yet?"

She plopped back on the bed, holding the pillow tight to her chest.

Noir gripped the knob and pulled open the door.

"Where's my daughter?" Anna shoved him aside. She gasped. "Tamsyn. This is crazy. You can't live here. This has gone on long enough." She turned, looking Noir up and down. "I don't believe your mother raised you to answer the door half-naked. It's rude."

"What's rude is you barging into my home, barking orders, at the crack of dawn." Noir slammed the door.

"Anna, what are you doing here?" Tamsyn tossed the pillow across the bed. She found it amusing that she wasn't at all embarrassed that Anna had come waltzing in right after passionate sex, but if it had been Carter or Weezer, she would have been three shades of red.

"I've come to collect you and bring you home." Anna glared. "Or haven't you seen the news yet this morning?"

"What are you talking about?" Noir snagged his cell from the nightstand. "Shit," he mumbled. "My dad's been trying to reach us. He wants us to call him or come to the house right away."

"What is Alison reporting in the news?" Tamsyn found the remote and pointed it at the television in the corner. It was an odd setup, but it worked so that you could see the TV from the sofa and the bed. It was the only way it worked when your living room was in your bedroom.

"My dad's on his way over. He saw Anna's car fly by." Noir tossed his cell to the bed. "I'd bet my mother isn't far behind." He sat on the bed, stretching out his legs, not bothering to put on a shirt.

That was kind of annoying because Tamsyn figured he did it on purpose.

"Get your things, Tamsyn and let's—"

"Shhhh. The cycle is about to repeat." Tamsyn sat on the corner of the bed.

Noir inched behind her, wrapping his arms around her waist and resting his chin on her shoulder.

Anna made a noise that sounded like she was about to vomit. It was a cross between a gag and a coughing fit.

Tamsyn didn't bother to look up. This was her space. Her new home. With the man she loved. Anna wasn't going to ruin that. If she wanted to be a part of Tamsyn's life, she was going to have to accept the relationship. It was that simple. Fred had said his piece, but ultimately, he respected and valued her enough not to push her out of his life.

Her only problem with Fred right now was how he was treating Weezer and Carter in this case.

"Turn it up," Noir said.

His parents busted through the door. Carter glared at Anna.

What started out as a great morning had turned into hell on earth.

"We're about to watch the news," Noir said. "We haven't seen it yet." He glanced up. "Can the three of you be nice to each other?"

"We can." Carter wrapped his arm around Weezer. It didn't appear as if he was protecting her, but more like keeping her from attacking.

"I'm going to make some coffee," Weezer said. "We've already seen the news."

"Tamsyn, really. We need to go," Anna whispered. "We'll talk in the car."

"I'm not going anywhere, so either make yourself comfortable or leave." Tamsyn hadn't meant to sound so brutal. She just wanted to get on with it. "Now, can everyone be quiet so I can unpause this thing?"

"We've obtained bank records," Alison said as images of canceled checks flashed on the screen next to her over-stated face and unnatural blond hair. *"...from an anonymous source that we've since validated that shows Carter River did indeed give money to Elizabeth Tuttle. This isn't a check here or there. This is at least one or two payouts a year for ten years. Why would Carter River be giving Elizabeth Tuttle money? Especially when it has been proven he's not Tamsyn's father."* The screen changed and the paternity test appeared.

"How the hell did she get that?" Tamsyn muttered. "The only people who have a copy are me and Carter."

"My copy is missing," Carter said. "We found that out when we went through my home office."

Tamsyn pointed the clicker and paused the TV. "You didn't tell me that, why?"

"That was one of the things I planned on talking to you two about this morning." Carter took the mug that Weezer offered and handed it to Anna.

That was nice.

But she shook her head, plopping herself in a seat at the table by the door, clutching her damn bag.

So Carter brought it to Tamsyn and she wasn't about to turn away caffeine.

She brought it to her lips and the hot liquid rolled past her throat and into her stomach. "Oh God. That's good. Thanks, Weezer."

"You're welcome, sweetheart."

Anna made some weird noise that sounded like she swore under her breath.

"Please, continue, Carter. I need to understand why you neglected to tell me something that is as important as that," Tamsyn said.

"That document is benign. It puts to rest a lot of questions and Alison had already made mention of it, so at first glance, it going missing could have been as simple as me filing it at my office instead of in my home. But I didn't do that either." Carter handed a mug to Noir and then made himself comfortable on the sofa with his back to Anna. "I still didn't think too hard on it. Again, it was a piece of news that shouldn't matter anymore. Until you put it in that context and add in your mother's remains being found on my property."

"Can we listen to the rest of the newscast and then discuss this?" Weezer asked. "In private."

"Tamsyn." Anna abruptly stood. "I'd like to go."

"You can leave, if you'd like," Tamsyn said.

"I need you to come with me." Anna's voice trembled. A tear dribbled down her cheek.

Tamsyn sucked in a deep breath, letting it out slowly. The tension in the air wrapped her body like a straitjacket. She rose, handing Noir her coffee. "I'm not going to leave this second. But how about I meet you in two hours for a late breakfast and we can talk then."

Anna took her hands and held them with a death grip. "I don't want you to stay here. Please, I'm begging you. Come with me."

"I'll see you at the diner." Tamsyn kissed Anna's cheek. "Two hours. I promise."

"Fine." Anna adjusted her bag.

"Don't forget we're decorating the main hall tonight for the showcase." Weezer glanced over her shoulder and smiled, although it was anything but sweet. "The Holiday Showcase is tomorrow. We have a lot of work cut out for us."

"I'll be there." Anna nodded. "Don't you be late, honey." Anna squeezed Tamsyn's hands. She turned on her heel and stomped out the door in a huff.

"She's so exhausting sometimes," Tamsyn mumbled.

"You handled her beautifully." Weezer's smile settled into a warm and caring one. "I'll admit I was a little surprised to see her drive down the road, but this news coverage is all hype, not substance, and it's not going to make things nice for any of us."

"I can see where it's going." Tamsyn returned to her seat, grabbed her mug, and hit the play button on the remote.

"We all know Carter River helped his daughter-in-law and her mother disappear twenty-two years ago. He has money,

means, and connections to make things happen. While he's done some incredible things for this community, like help get rid of corruption in the sheriff's office, there is no doubt in anyone's mind that he and his wife have also done some questionable things. Could it be possible that Carter had this document forged and he paid for his mistress' silence?"

"You've got to be fucking kidding me." Noir slammed his mug on the nightstand and stood. He paced between the bed and the sofa, raking his fingers through his hair. "That's just irresponsible reporting."

"I've already called the station as well as the lab that did the paternity test. She's going to have to retract," Carter said. "And it will be before the end of the day. The lab would also do a rush and we could get the results today. I know it doesn't feel this way for the two of you, but it will be more embarrassing for Alison than you."

"I'm less worried what people are think about that." Tamsyn sipped her coffee. "The real issue is explaining those checks." She held up her hand. "We all know my mom slept with a lot of men. I'm sure she slept with a few people in this town that were married. Just because you're not my father, that doesn't mean you didn't have an affair. That right there changes the focus of what Weezer's fight with my mom was all about. It makes it less about me and more about an ongoing affair. Like you were taking care of your mistress for years. It doesn't matter who my father is; what matters is that you had a sidepiece."

"My lawyer—God, that sounds strange to say that—is filing a motion to see your mother's bank accounts," Carter said. "Every time I gave your mother money, it was for something specific. Medical bills for you. Rent. A few times she got herself into trouble. If you look at my checks, they are for specific amounts. I didn't round up. I didn't give her extra. I also made sure she used the money for what it was meant for. We want to match those dates with anything she might have paid."

"And you have an accounting of that?" Tamsyn asked.

"I do." Carter ran a hand over his unshaven face. "But that file was where your paternity test was. It was in my home office in a filing cabinet that is locked when I'm not home." He cocked his head. "The only people who know where I keep the key are my kids and Weezer."

"But the file was labeled, correct?" Tamsyn asked.

"Yes." Carter nodded.

"Any chance you can get me a list of those people who have been in your house—including family—for the last two weeks?"

Carter leaned over and pulled out a piece of paper from his back pocket. "Already done. It's a short list, mostly including a few staff members and the Holiday Showcase committee," he said. "And before I forget, Richard Berkin is not your father. That came back last night."

"While it would have been nice to have a sister, I

have to admit, I'm glad not to be related to that bastard," she mumbled. "Fred will get pissed off, but I'm going to make a statement about paternity. I'm the one who asked you to do it. I'm the one who went to the lab. I'm putting that fucker to rest once and for all." Tamsyn cringed. "I apologize for my language."

"There is a time and a place for everything," Weezer said. "And fuck is appropriate right now. But do you think that's a good idea? Especially since that little witch Alison could very well get her hands on the paternity test you just did, which shows you're actively seeking your biological father. That could put a whole different spin on this that we're not even considering."

"That's a risk I need to take." She stood next to Noir, taking his hand, squeezing hard.

He glanced at her with a confused expression.

"With your permission, I want to give the statement right here in front of the cottage," Tamsyn said.

"First, you live here. If that's what you want to do, we can't stop you," Carter said. "But why would you want to bring the news media here? Bringing that kind of attention to where your mother's body was found, especially when the police have barricaded the access road because it leads to two private residences."

"This is your property and I want to be respectful. If—"

Carter waved his hand. "You can give a statement to the press from the cottage, if that's what you want. I just want to know why."

"I need you to trust me; can you do that?" She glanced between Noir and his parents.

Noir wrapped his arm around her waist. "I know I can."

"So can we," Weezer said. "That brings us to a different subject." She recrossed her legs, sitting up taller. "Can the two of you please sit down?"

"Sure." Noir took her by the hand, guiding her back to the bed.

That felt a little strange, but the entire morning had been weird.

She sat cross-legged with her fingers intertwined with Noir's.

"This is an odd time to bring it up, but since we're already speaking to an architect, we thought we needed to have a chat with the two of you," Carter said.

"I'm not following, Dad," Noir said.

"This cottage is too small for two people and the main house is too big for your mom and me." Carter smiled. "All your other siblings have settled into beautiful homes. None of them are going to give up where they are and move back into the family home and it's time for your mom and me to give it up."

"And go where, exactly?" Noir asked.

"Here. But not until after we've added a few extra bedrooms for when grandkids come to visit. A bigger kitchen. A den for myself. But we sure as shit don't need a six-thousand-square-foot home," Carter said. "We'd like you and Tamsyn to have it." He held out his hand. "Now, it will be about six months before construction on this place would be done, and I doubt you want to live with us, so we've taken the liberty to ask Chablis and Dax about their garage apartment. You can stay there while we rebuild the cottage."

Tamsyn's body went numb. She couldn't feel her toes. Her fingers. And her brain did not function. It registered the words, but she couldn't store them. On the one hand, she comprehended that Carter and Weezer were giving their son a home. A different place to live.

She remembered when Toby and Zinny moved into Carter's other house. The one that had belonged to his parents. It had been a gift. A generous one. And Carter helped out all his kids in different ways, depending on where they needed it.

Dax and Chablis didn't need money. Neither did Trey and Reisling. But Carter was still generous.

However, Tamsyn wasn't a member of this family, and she shouldn't be part of this discussion. "I should excuse myself." She planted her feet on the floor.

Noir curled his fingers around her wrist. "Dad, why don't Tamsyn and I stay here after the renovation. The main house is your home. You've lived in it forever."

"We're too old to take care of it," Weezer said. "It needs youth. Energy." She leaned over and took her son's hand. And then Tamsyn's. "It needs a couple that's going to fill it with children."

Tamsyn coughed. "That's putting the big old cart before a very tiny horse."

Weezer laughed. "Are you moving in with my son or not?"

"Well, yes." Tamsyn narrowed her eyes.

"Do you love my son?" Weezer lowered her chin.

"I do." Tamsyn swallowed. Hard.

"Okay, then. Wedding bells are just around the corner." Weezer patted her cheek.

"That's going a little too far, Mom." Noir eased off the bed. "Are you sure this is what you want to do?"

"We are." Carter pulled Noir close, giving him a big hug. "We love you, son. That house is yours, if you want it. We'll talk more about it later."

"Come on, old man. We have a busy day of preparing for the Holiday Showcase and dealing with idiots who like to gossip. Let's go." She damn near hoisted Carter off the sofa.

He grabbed their coats, helping his wife with hers before pushing his arms through his. "We'll be in touch. Let us know if anything happens with the case, okay?"

She flung herself backward on the bed. "Oh my God. Your parents are insane."

"You don't want to live in my childhood home?" He sprawled out next to her, resting his arm on her middle.

"Not even the point. It's so very presumptuous—"

He pressed his finger over her lips. "That might be

214

true, but they are right. I love you and sooner or later we will get married."

She blinked. "Are you proposing? Because that would freak me out more than everything else that's happening."

"No. It is way too soon for that." He kissed her shoulder. "But I have thought about our future. There isn't anyone else for me. I love you and I wish I could make all this go away. I can't stand to see you hurting."

"You're a sweet man and I'm going to need you to trust me." She rolled. "I'm going to get Fred to let me work the Holiday Showcase. It's going to be awkward and I have the feeling that things might get worse for your parents, but no matter what happens, I need you to not listen to the words that come out of my mouth." She pressed her hand to his chest. "Hear your heart. Please. Can you do that?"

"I've ignored my heart half my life. I'm not going to do that anymore."

Tamsyn had no idea if her plan would work to flesh out whoever was trying to set up Carter and Weezer, but she hoped she didn't lose her boyfriend in the process.

Tamsyn

"I want to work the showcase." Tamsyn squared her shoulders, holding Fred's gaze.

"After the stunt you pulled today? I have half a mind to suspend you." Fred folded his arms across his chest and leaned back. "What the hell were you thinking? Giving a statement is one thing. I have no issue with you cleaning up the shitshow that's your paternity. But to do it at The River Winery? Where your mother's body was found? Are you trying to stir the pot? What could you seriously have to gain by doing that?"

"I have my reasons."

"I'd like to hear them." He lifted his chin. "Or are you going to give me more BS like you gave Anna at breakfast? Because all she wants for you is to be happy, and all you did was dig your heels into the ground like a toddler."

Tamsyn laughed. "Are you serious? This morning, yours and Anna's sole purpose was to get me to break up with Noir."

Fred raised his palm. "My words were to put the relationship on pause until this crisis is over." He lowered his chin. "Anna might come at things sideways, but she means well."

"Maybe so, but there's no way I'm going to call it quits with Noir."

"I'm not asking you to," Fred said. "However, living there isn't a good look for you or this department. You can put that on hold and public appearances with Noir. That's the responsible thing to do."

Not if she was going to catch whoever wanted to frame Weezer and Carter.

Fred leaned forward, opening a desk drawer. "I really didn't want to tell you this way, but the full autopsy report on your mom is back and it's as we suspected." He pushed it across the table.

"Does Anna know about this? Is this why her panties are in a wad?" With tentative fingers, Tamsyn lifted the folder. She took a quick glance over the pages. Her heart hammered in her throat.

A feather pendant had been found with the body.

That made no fucking sense.

"Anna doesn't know the details, but yes, she's aware. It's going to be public knowledge in fifteen minutes."

All the more reason for Tamsyn to go ahead with her plans. Part of her wanted to trust Fred. Tell him about the necklace. About her thoughts regarding this being her biological father. The problem with doing that was she had no motive. She didn't understand what grudge her real father might have with the Rivers. She needed the backdrop of the Holiday Showcase to set her plan in motion. She needed to see the reactions of the townspeople.

And she needed—no, wait. Maybe she didn't need to be in uniform to do that.

"Are you going to let me work the showcase or not?"

"No," Fred said with a furrowed brow. "You're not

going to ask me about that report?"

"I don't need to. My mother was murdered. Gunshot to the head. Close range." She glanced down. "The body had also been moved. It makes no sense for Carter and Weezer to unearth my mother and move her to a new location—on their property no less."

"I'm going to a judge for a warrant to see if their weapons match that of the one that took your mother's life."

Tamsyn tossed the file on the desk. "That will still be circumstantial. We both know that Weezer had two registered shotguns. Carter had two as well. He has a permit to carry a pistol. I can name twenty people in this town who carry the exact same one. That would include you and Silas."

"Jesus, Tamsyn. You have a right to that report. But I'm pulling your access." Fred snatched the file and stuffed it back in the drawer. "You're blinded by whatever emotions you have for Noir and they're clouding your judgment."

"Carter and Weezer are good people. They didn't hurt my mother."

Fred let out an audible sigh. "I don't for one second believe Carter could hurt a fly." Fred held up his hand. "Unless his family was attacked, and then all bets are off. But that's true of most good men. But Weezer? That woman is a loose cannon. There are things we've uncovered that I haven't shared with you and it all points back to Weezer."

Tamsyn's muscles tightened. She couldn't believe the words that were tumbling out of Fred's mouth. What Kool-Aid was he drinking? It was utterly ridiculous. "You seriously can't believe that?"

"We both know I have to go where the evidence points." He cocked his head. "And no, you can't see it. If you warn the River family where this is going, I will have your badge."

"I know better." She bit her tongue.

Fred was a better cop—a better investigator—than this. She had to wonder if this was his way of pissing her off to either keep her away, or to keep her digging on her own, without causing waves within the department or with State.

She wanted to give him the benefit of the doubt, but that was damn hard considering the scowl he sported. "I will respect the investigation and your wishes, but I won't give up my boyfriend."

"I wish you'd reconsider."

"May I be excused?"

"Of course." Fred nodded.

She stepped outside into the hallway. There was a fine line between what she could tell Carter and Weezer regarding the case and what she planned on doing. Even then, it might not work. She ran the risk of spooking whoever was behind the setup, but it was a risk she believed she had to take.

Time to play ball.

14

NOIR

"Wow." Noir stood in the middle of the cottage and stared at the most intoxicating woman in the world.

Tamsyn wore a red dress that came down to the middle of her shins. It was low-cut, showing off way too much of her cleavage. He liked it, but he didn't want the rest of Candlewood Falls enjoying it. The sleeves were off the shoulders and quarter-length.

Her heels were sparkly and at least three inches.

She wore her hair partially up. The rest was in big curls, falling over her bare shoulders.

Stunning was an understatement.

"You like it?"

"Um, yeah, but I'm wondering if we have time for me to rip it off your body and—"

"No. We don't." She laughed. "Besides, we've

already had our fun this morning, or have you already forgotten?"

"Oh, I haven't. But that makes me want to do it again."

She rolled her eyes. "You're a horndog."

"I won't deny it, but it's your fault. You're too sexy."

"Oh my God. That's such a line." She held out her hand, her mother's feather pendant dangling from her fingertips.

"What the hell are you doing?" He took it and glared. "Why on earth would you wear this?"

"To see what kind of reaction I get from people in town." She turned. "I'm guessing my biological father might react to it. Now, could you please help me put it on?"

"That's a dangerous game. Someone planted that in our cottage."

"I love how you call it ours."

"Don't be cute," he said as he clasped the necklace. "Does your wearing this have anything to do with asking my parents to meet us before the showcase?"

"Yes and no." She took his hand. "That box your parents found with my mother's things. They only knew one item."

"The bracelet my mom gave to yours." Noir fingered the pendant dangling close to Tamsyn's breast. "There was also a picture of you and your mom in that box. That clinched it for them, because that bracelet wasn't one of a kind. It wasn't expensive."

"That's true. But my mom didn't wear that bracelet often. As a matter of fact, almost never. She was saving it for me. She told me that someone special had given it to her the day I was born and she figured it was meant for me."

"You didn't know it came from my mom?" Noir had never seen it before, nor had he ever known of its existence. But it did sound like something his mom would do. She would even ask not to be mentioned.

"Nope. But here's the thing. I would have known about that bracelet and every other item in that box. I also would know about this pendant, though no one else would because my mom almost never wore it and she told me not to talk about where the necklace came from. It was our secret. I started to get excited on the days she wore it because I believed she was going to see my father. She was wearing it the day she went missing."

"You're sure about that?"

"I'm positive." Tamsyn pursed her lips.

Noir ran his hand up and down her arm. "My dad told me she emptied her bank accounts."

"I struggle with that one, because it makes it look as though she was leaving me. My mother was a lot of things, but she'd never abandon me." Tamsyn took her coat off the rack. "I was only ten. However, I remember her acting strange. Not bad strange, but nervous. And a little giddy, which looking back, seems so off because of that fight with Weezer and the accusations my mom hurled at Carter, which weren't true."

"Have you ever talked to my dad about this? Or Fred?" Noir opened the door and helped her down the freshly shoveled path. It was too cold and snowy to walk, so they would drive over to the winery. It wasn't that far, but it made the most sense.

"No. Not really."

"Why not?" Noir opened the car door, helping Tamsyn into the passenger seat, lifting her dress so it didn't touch the snow. "They might have some insight."

"I have my reasons and I need you to trust me."

"I do, I just don't understand." He closed the door and jogged around the hood. Slipping behind the wheel, he pressed the start button. The engine roared to life. He hit the gas, easing down the drive. "My folks will meet us in my mom's office in the winery. They don't have much time. Anna and Mrs. Cummings are making my mom nuts. Mrs. Cummings is once again dressed as Mrs. Claus and my mom wants to rip the damn costume off her."

Tamsyn laughed. "She dresses like that every year."

Noir parked on the side of the building where deliveries took place. It had been roped off to the public. He guided Tamsyn through the back door. No one would see them come in the winery. He took Tamsyn's hand and led her through the gift shop, which wouldn't be open until after the showcase. They climbed the staircase to his mom's office.

His gut twisted. He did trust Tamsyn. She was his world. The air that he breathed. He'd be lost without her, but not knowing the extent of her plan made him nervous. She might have a gun strapped to her leg, but going rogue made her dangerous.

Perhaps not in a good way.

He was going to have to find a way to talk with his dad in private.

"You have ten minutes," his mom said at the top of the stairs. She waved them into her office.

His father leaned against the desk. "Son." He nodded. "Tamsyn. You look beautiful this evening."

"Thank you." Tamsyn shed her coat, resting it on the back of one of the chairs before sitting in it. "I appreciate you meeting with me before the showcase started."

"I only agreed because you said it was important." His mom closed the door. "I have to say, you look stunning in that dress." She smiled. "Now, what can we do for you? Because I need to get back to the ballroom before Anna takes over my show."

Tamsyn fiddled with the pendant.

Shit. Was she trying to get a reaction from his parents? What the fuck kind of game was she playing?

Noir shifted his gaze between his parents.

His dad hadn't moved from his spot on the desk. He looked relaxed. When he felt backed into a corner, his facial muscles tightened. He folded his arms across his chest. Or he paced.

He did none of those things.

His mother sat next to Tamsyn and looked at her intently, waiting patiently for Tamsyn to speak. But there wasn't a hint of recognition. She didn't appear to be fazed.

His mother wasn't a good actress, contrary to popular belief. She was dramatic. Over the top. But she wore her emotions on her sleeve.

"I'm going to tell you a couple of things that I could lose my job over," Tamsyn said.

His mom rested her hand on Tamsyn's leg. "I don't want you to do that."

"Me neither," his dad said. "We understand that you're in a difficult situation. But don't put your career in jeopardy for us. We're well aware that come tomorrow, we'll be taken in for official questioning."

"Fred's taken away my access," Tamsyn said. "As far as this case is concerned, I'm the family member. I'll be told what's going on, but I won't be able to see anything. The last piece of information I saw was the autopsy report."

"Fred executed a warrant earlier today for our weapons," his mom said. "He told us your mom was murdered. He didn't give us any details other than a gunshot."

"There was something in the autopsy report that doesn't make sense to me. There was something found with the body that belonged to my mother that was so personal, but last week, I found that same item stuffed in the cottage bathroom medicine cabinet."

"You haven't told anyone about that," his father said. "Which doesn't help us. It actually hurts."

"Yes and no," Tamsyn said.

"What is the item?" his mother asked.

"You don't know?" Noir narrowed his stare, studying his mother for any hint of recognition.

"I wouldn't be asking if I knew." His mom cocked her head.

"I take it you know." His father pushed from the desk and strolled toward the window that overlooked the gift shop. "On the one hand, whatever this item is, you having it could be the thing that proves we had nothing to do with your mom's murder. Or it could be the thing that allows someone to set us up for something we didn't do."

"I believe it's both," Tamsyn said.

"This is a dangerous game and I don't like it." Noir plopped himself in the big leather chair. "Can you please just tell us whatever it is you have planned."

"I one hundred percent believe neither one of you had anything to do with my mother's death. I do believe that my biological father did and I think he's going to be here tonight."

"Wait a second." His father turned. "No one on our potential list will be here tonight." He held up his hand. "And why on earth would there be two items?"

"I have two different theories on that," Tamsyn said. "He has an accomplice and they didn't communicate. Or we have two different crimes for two different reasons." She held up the pendant. "This was my mother's. Although, I don't know if this one was hers or the one found with the body. The point is, I need a little help gauging people's reactions and since my instincts tell me you've never seen this before, and the three of you are the only people I trust, I need you to keep your eyes and ears open. If anyone—"

"We need more than just us." His mom took both of Tamsyn's hands. "My son loves you. So do we. And so does everyone else in this family. You're part of us. This is bigger than finding out who is setting us up. This is about finding who killed your mother. Let us enlist the rest of the family."

Noir leaned forward. "My mom's right. We can add Tamsyn to the adult family text string. Mom's going to be busy with the showcase, but the rest of us will be wandering and chatting with everyone; we can be your eyes and ears."

"I don't know. The more people who know what—"

"Tamsyn. Let us help you." His dad pulled out his cell. "Whoever is doing this will assume we're so busy with the Holiday Showcase they could easily believe it's the perfect time to put the final touches on their plan."

"You're going to pull the rest of your kids in whether I want you to or not, aren't you?" Tamsyn asked.

"Yes," his dad said. "While finding out who killed your mom is priority number one, I'm not letting my wife go to prison for something she didn't do. Not on my watch."

"I don't like any of this." Noir rubbed his temples. "Especially the part that puts Tamsyn in the middle of a cat and mouse game."

"Son, she's a cop. It's what she does," his mother said.

Noir sighed. Every morning she walked out that door in her uniform, he worried. But this was different. Now his entire family was in jeopardy and his mom's freedom hung in the balance.

Tamsyn

The Holiday Showcase had winded down and Tamsyn had lost hope in finding her biological father, who murdered her mother, and who set up the Rivers. She snagged her glass of wine and took a big gulp as a few more guests shuffled out of the winery.

Anna had been busy all night acting as if she'd saved the showcase. It had been comical to watch and if Tamsyn hadn't been so preoccupied, it would have been funny. Fred had been avoiding her all evening. He hadn't even said hello and that pissed her off. There was no reason for him to do that. She didn't care that they were at odds professionally. Maybe even personally.

He wanted them to be a family.

But he wasn't acting that way.

"Hey." Eddy, her colleague, strolled over. "I have some bad news for you."

"Not sure I want to hear it."

"You need to," Eddy said. "I shouldn't be telling you, but Fred's making the wrong call."

"Why? What's he doing?"

"He's going to arrest Weezer after everyone leaves."

"For what?" Tamsyn set her drink on the table.

"Murder," Eddy said flatly.

"That's insane. He doesn't have enough evidence to do that. Sure, he can haul her down for questioning as a person of interest, but there isn't enough evidence to warrant an arrest."

"He says he got the smoking gun during the last search."

"That's bullshit." She scanned the room. Fred stood in the back corner. In fucking uniform. When did he do that? Asshole. "Excuse me."

Eddy curled his fingers around her forearm. "Don't do it."

"Let go of me." She jerked her arm free and marched—more like wobbled in her high heels—toward Fred. Nothing was going to stop her from having words with her boss. She reached up and grabbed the pendant as if to give her luck. "What the hell do you think you're doing?"

Fred lowered his chin. "Excuse me?"

"You can't arrest Weezer. That's wrong." She held the pendant so tight she worried it might break.

Fred's face hardened. He narrowed his eyes. "We're not having this discussion here. Actually, we're not having it all."

She dropped her hand to her side. "Oh, yes, we are. I might not have seen all the evidence, but I know a few things."

His jaw dropped open. His gaze went from her necklace to her face and back to her necklace. His eyes widened with a hint of recognition.

He knew what it was. He'd seen it when they pulled her mother's body from the shallow grave.

"I don't have time for your antics right now," he said behind tight lips. "You're too emotionally involved. I want you to stay out of this and Eddy is in deep shit for telling you anything. Don't you dare warn anyone. Get out of here. Let me do my job." He turned on his heel and left her standing there.

She dug into her purse and quickly sent a text to the River family. Yeah, she wasn't going to stay quiet. Once that was done, she raced off after Fred. That conversation was far from over.

Fred had slinked out the side door, leading toward the path that went to the vineyard.

But he wasn't alone. He had Anna with him—more like he was dragging her down the path.

What the hell?

God, she wished she weren't in heels.

Her first instinct was to race to them and continue confronting Fred until she got her answers. But she didn't like the way he manhandled Anna. She'd never seen that before. Anna ruled the roost.

It had always been *yes, dear, whatever you want, dear.* He cowered to her and gave her whatever she wanted. He almost never raised his voice to her and he never laid a hand on her.

Ever.

This seemed over the top, and most certainly out of place.

She slinked up the side of the path, hiding herself in the trees. She needed to get close enough to them so she could hear their hushed voices without being seen.

"Have you seen Tamsyn tonight?" Fred asked Anna.

"I have and I can't believe she didn't take the bait. That she didn't immediately call you when she found the necklace. Maybe she doesn't remember it was her mother's."

Holy shit. Tamsyn swallowed. She needed backup. And fast. She fumbled with the clasp on her purse, finding her phone, and she texted Eddy, giving him her location.

"Why didn't you tell me you did that?" Fred held Anna by the shoulders and shook her.

"You told me to plant things in the house. I did that."

"Not the necklace. Never the necklace. She was wearing that when she disappeared. It was on the body when we recovered it. And seriously, Anna. A shallow grave? On the winery? I told you to let me handle that. I told you I would take care of everything and now I've got to clean up your mess. Again. If you had listened to me and let me deal with moving the body and everything else, this wouldn't be such a shitshow."

Tears burned a path down Tamsyn's frozen cheeks. She stepped from the shadows. "You killed my mother. You moved her body and tried to frame the Rivers. Why?" She stood ten paces away, staring at the two people who had told her they wanted to be a family. That they loved her like their own.

Nothing in her world made sense.

Fred spun on his heel. He drew his gun.

And pointed it at her.

"Tamsyn, this isn't what you think," Fred said, weapon still raised.

"Really? Because I've been listening to the two of you talk about planting evidence on this winery. Moving my mother's body. Please explain yourself."

Anna inched behind Fred, hiding her face.

"Where's your gun?" Fred took three steps forward, his hand steady. His eyes were filled with rage, something she'd never seen before. "I know you're always carrying. So hand it over, and then we're going for a walk."

"What are you going to do? Kill me too?"

"Just fucking do it."

Tamsyn reached under her dress. With tentative fingers, she unholstered her weapon. For a split second she thought about a standoff. But she needed more time for Eddy to arrive. More time to get answers.

"Put it on the ground and kick it over."

She did as instructed. "Why did you plant the necklace? All the items in the Rivers' home? The body? And why would you kill my mother?" There were more questions, but those were a good start.

Fred snatched the gun, handing it to Anna. "Let's go for a walk." He shoved his weapon into her side and pushed her forward.

She stumbled.

"I have a right to know, regardless of what you're going to do with me."

"Fred," Anna whispered. "I'm sorry. I didn't realize. I thought I was helping. You had so many other things to handle."

"What's done is done," Fred said. "Now we'll have to deal with it and maybe it will work to our advantage."

"How?" Anna asked.

"My little girl isn't stupid. If she wore the necklace, she has no idea it was found on her mother's body. And she certainly wouldn't have informed Carter or Weezer."

Little girl? Tamsyn swallowed. Of all the people who could have been her father, Fred was not someone she ever thought could fit the bill. She filed that in the back of her brain for the moment.

"Besides, lots of people could have that necklace," Fred said. "You made a grave error in judgment and it's going to cost you your life, Weezer her freedom, and Carter his entire world."

Well, that certainly spelled out Fred's plan. But it didn't explain why. And she needed those answers. "Why would you want to do that? Please, Fred. I'm begging you to tell me because it doesn't make sense. Carter's your friend. He helped you become police chief."

"Fred, you can't be serious? You can't kill her. Not after all these years. Not after what I did for you. The secret I've kept all these years. The betrayal I've had to live with. And the truth is I've come to care for her," Anna said through her tears.

"Anna, if you had just let me handle it, we wouldn't be in this mess."

"Are you kidding me?" Anna stopped. "You've been telling me for years you'd handle Weezer and Carter. But you never have. She still acts like she's fucking queen of this town. She has made my life miserable. But ever since Carter got you this job, you've backed off, forgetting that he didn't back you the first time you wanted to go for chief of police. Forgetting that he treated you like you were less of a man than—"

"Be quiet, Anna," Fred said.

Tamsyn blinked. "The first time?"

"Yeah. Your father wanted the job when Harper was appointed. The mayor at the time was torn and Carter had his ear. He didn't believe your dad was ready. Said he was soft. Didn't have what it took to be a leader." Anna stepped from behind Fred's back. "At every turn, Carter and Weezer have been destroying our dreams. I thought I had it locked up when we got Elizabeth to agree to accuse Carter. We had all the checks that Carter had paid her. We had documentation of all the times he visited her. We had the fight. We were going to unearth your mother years ago, but then your dad got cold feet. He wanted to raise you. He made me look at his indiscretion day in and day out. A constant reminder of my failings as a woman. I didn't want to, but I'm a kind and forgiving woman and I wasn't going to let Carter and Weezer raise you. But over the years, I grew to care for you, so I let the mystery of what happened to your mother stay buried. I did that for you."

"That wasn't for me. That was for yourself." Tamsyn couldn't believe the crap that had come from Anna's mouth. The realization that all the answers to her questions had been right under her nose hit her soul like a freight train. "You're my fucking father." Tamsyn shook her head. "All these years I've wanted two things and both of you knew the answers. Un-fucking-believable. How dare you deceive me like this? And you want to frame two innocent people because you don't like them."

"Oh, it goes so much deeper than that, darling," Anna said.

"It doesn't matter." Fred shoved his gun deeper in her side, pushing her along the path toward the overflow cabin. "We're going to prove that Carter paid off the lab that did the paternity test. Once you're dead, I'm going to have another one done and prove that he's your father. I'm going to prove he killed your mother."

"I can almost buy that, but no one is going to believe he moved my mother's body." Tamsyn shivered. Why hadn't Eddy shown up yet?

"That's where I'm going to have to get creative. But I think I'll find evidence out here that she was originally in the overflow building. He and Weezer tried to move the body when you and Noir started dating. That was a little close for comfort and—"

"You do realize that you're going to put out a false statement that I've been sleeping with my half brother." No way was Tamsyn going to let that lie out in the world again.

"I'm going to enjoy watching this family suffer," Fred said. "They honestly believe they are above the law. They have gotten away with so much shit and I'm tired of having to sit back and watch it happen. I honestly thought I'd have some power as chief of police, but Carter fucking runs this town." Fred glanced around. He pointed his weapon at the door to the overflow building and fired.

It might be a big vineyard, but someone was bound to hear that.

She hoped.

Otherwise, she was about to join her mother in the afterlife.

But the music still pouring out of the speakers from the winery killed any hope she had.

15

CARTER

"Have you seen Tamsyn?" Carter took Weezer to the side of the room.

"Not in the last fifteen minutes or so. Why?"

"Fred changed into his uniform." Carter raked his fingers through his hair. "If that wasn't nerve-racking enough, Fred, Anna, and Tamsyn have all disappeared. I can't find any of them anywhere in this building."

"Where's Noir?"

"He and Dax are checking the labeling room and other places we're not allowing the public to go. Malbec and Nebbiolo are in the parking lot. Toby and Trey have planted themselves at both exits. All the girls are doing their best to say goodbye to the rest of the guests. Something isn't right."

"Tell me about it. There are three cop cars outside."

"Besides that." Carter pulled his cell from his sports

coat pocket. There were no texts from Tamsyn, and that was disconcerting as well. "I think we need to—"

"Mr. River." Eddy, a colleague of Tamsyn, strolled across the room, his fingers laced in his belt, definitely in cop mode.

Wonderful.

"Yes?" Carter squared his shoulders, bracing for the worst. Although, he couldn't imagine that Fred would send this young man to arrest his wife. Then again, Fred could be a coward. It was one of the reasons that Carter had pushed hard twenty years ago not to have Fred as the chief of police. The only reason he'd backed him this last time was because he thought Fred had changed. That and he was the lesser of two evils, so to speak.

At the moment, Carter was questioning that decision.

Eddy glanced over his shoulder. "I have a situation." He held up his cell. "I think Tamsyn's in trouble. Where's Noir?"

"He's in the back room. What's going on?"

"I'm not exactly sure, but I also don't think I can bring in my department. Or at least all of them. We've been instructed to clear the winery, except not to let you leave."

"I gathered something was going on."

"But Tamsyn chased Fred outside and she sent me that text and I'm worried. I don't know what to do.

Fred's my boss. Tamsyn's my partner. This isn't necessarily a police matter."

Carter took the cell.

Tamsyn: *Come to this location. Come alone. Be prepared to call for backup. Hurry. Come with an open mind.*

"Fuck," Carter muttered. "Do you have any extra weapons? Because your boss took all of mine."

"I don't like that question," Eddy said.

"What's going on?" Weezer asked.

"I can't believe I didn't see this." Carter texted the family to meet him in the labeling room. "Let's walk." He turned, moving the barricade to the back of the winery building. "Weezer and I have thought that Anna might have planted that box of items in our china cabinet."

"Why would she do that?" Eddy asked.

"Outside of hating my wife, I couldn't figure that out. But then Tamsyn told us she found something else in the cottage. She'd been holding on to it, not telling anyone. She thought it would help her find her father. I believe she just did."

Weezer gasped. "No. Fred? But he can't have kids? He and Anna tried for years. Anna always said he was the problem."

"I bet it was her, not Fred." Carter paused at the door to the wine labeling room. "It makes sense as to why Fred went so easy on Elizabeth. She was the mother to his kid. But Elizabeth once told me that Tamsyn's father was going to take care of them. That he was going to come back to her and take them away. That's the part that doesn't make sense to me."

Weezer placed her hand on his shoulder. "We have to find them. If she figured it out, they're going to feel backed into a corner and who knows what they will do."

"That's what I'm afraid of."

Tamsyn

Tamsyn stepped into the overflow building. "I need to know a few more things." She hugged her body. "You at least owe me that before you put a bullet in my head."

"We don't owe you anything," Anna said. "We gave you everything. We took you into our home. We raised you. And you couldn't even appreciate that. All you've ever done is shit on us. When the rumors about Carter resurfaced, you went behind our backs and got a paternity test. How do you think that made us feel?"

Tamsyn ignored the rant. "How long have you known you were my father?" She stared at Fred.

"Your entire life." He leaned against a stack of wine boxes, his weapon pointed at the center of her chest. Fred was a good shot. Not great, but he wouldn't miss at this range.

"I thought it was you who couldn't have children," Tamsyn said.

"That's the story we told so that no one would ever think it was my husband who fathered you." Anna wiped at her cheeks. "I was so devastated that he cheated on me and with Elizabeth. She was a vile woman."

Tamsyn glared. She wanted to lunge forward and squeeze the life out of Anna. "You said she was your friend."

"Never. She blackmailed your father for years. She threatened to tell everyone the truth if he didn't give her child support. We couldn't afford to write her checks, but we quietly did other things."

"Like what?" Tamsyn couldn't fill her lungs. Everything she thought about her life had been a sham. Her teenage years flashed before her eyes. The feelings of not fitting in rumbled in her gut. She thought it had been about missing her mom, when in reality, it had all been because they hadn't wanted her. But why did they keep her?

"I didn't arrest her when I could. I let her drug dealer off with a warning. I made sure CPS didn't take you away. Anything I could think of to keep her from talking," Fred said.

"When your father saw that Carter was giving Elizabeth money, we knew what we had to do. We made sure everyone would believe the rumors, and we told

Elizabeth if she didn't go along with it, you'd be taken from her."

"That's just cruel." Bile smacked the back of Tamsyn's throat.

"So is blackmail," Anna said. "But your mother got cold feet. She decided she wasn't going to go along with the plan."

"So, you killed her." Tears poured like a raging waterfall from Tamsyn's eyes. "Why did you take me in? Why didn't you let me go into the system if you didn't want me?"

Anna laughed. "Because if we didn't, the fucking Rivers would have and we couldn't let them win."

"Win?" Tamsyn stumbled backward, toppling over a case of wine. She braced herself with her hands, landing hard on her wrist. She groaned, feeling the bone snap.

Neither Fred nor Anna did anything to help.

"Win? You see me as some prize." She rolled to her knees, using her good hand to push herself to her wobbly feet. "I'm a fucking person. And back then, I was a child." She pointed to Fred. "I'm your daughter and you saw me as a game? You didn't want me because you loved me."

"I never said that." For the first time since Fred had taken her hostage, he faltered. "Of course I care about you."

"But you don't love me. Not like a father should."

She held her limp wrist, doing her best not to focus on the throbbing pain.

"I asked Elizabeth to give you up. To let Anna and me adopt you," Fred said. "But Elizabeth wouldn't, and Anna wasn't ready to forgive me."

"Which one of you pulled the trigger?" Tamsyn asked with a shaky voice.

"Does it matter?" Fred asked.

"Yes," Tamsyn said.

"If you must know, Anna did. But I was there." Fred held her gaze. "Your mother wanted to back out of our deal. She didn't like hurting Carter and Weezer. She no longer believed we'd follow through with our end of the bargain."

"Which was what, exactly?" Tamsyn couldn't imagine what had been going through her mother's mind, but whatever it was, her mom had been a victim. She'd been taken advantage of by people who didn't care about anything but keeping their secrets.

"We had promised her security. Financial freedom," Fred said. "A ticket out of town."

"That's why she emptied her bank accounts," Tamsyn whispered.

"She was supposed to take you and leave town, but she changed her mind and she was going to tell everyone what she did. I couldn't let that happen," Anna said. "It would have destroyed Fred's good name."

"You're both crazy," Tamsyn said. "You're not going to get away with this."

"I already have," Fred said.

"Earlier, you mentioned I was smart. That I wouldn't have told Weezer and Carter. Well, you're right. I am smart, which is why I've told them everything. And I mean, everything," Tamsyn said.

"I don't believe you." Fred held his weapon steady. "And this conversation is over."

Noir

"Why are you all still standing here? We need to get out there. Let's go!" Noir raced into the labeling room. He'd just been there ten minutes ago.

"Calm down, son," his father said.

"The fuck I will. Not after that text you just sent. And why the hell wouldn't you send it to the regular family group message? The one that includes Tamsyn. If she's in trouble, she should know—"

"Because if Fred's smart, he'll take her phone, and then he'll know what we're up to." His dad squeezed his shoulder.

Eddy strolled through the door with two officers. "Carter, you're going to have to let us do this."

"You can do the cop part. But my family is going

with you whether you like it or not." His dad folded his arms across his chest, daring Eddy to challenge him.

"I can't have the entire clan out there, especially him." Eddy pointed to Noir.

"Oh, he's going," his dad said. "So am I. Malbec, Nebbiolo, and Merlot as well."

"We're wasting time." Merlot handed Noir a gun. "And before you say one word, these are all mine. All registered to me. No one is going to use them unless we need to. We'll let you go first, but we all consider Tamsyn family and I don't think I have to tell you what that means to us."

Eddy ran a hand across his face. "No, Merlot. You don't. But please don't make me arrest any of you."

"We'll try not to." Noir took the gun his brother handed him. Of all the kids in the family, Noir was the least likely to use a firearm. He'd grown up with weapons. He was a decent shot. He wasn't opposed to them, but because of his mother and her reputation, he'd always opted not to own one, unlike the rest of his family, right down to Zinny. He pulled up his cell. "According to the location of her phone, she's some-where in the middle of the vineyard."

His dad leaned in. "That looks like it could be the overflow building."

"I think it's time to tear that fucking place down and build a new one," his mother muttered. "Too many secrets were buried there. Too much pain."

"I couldn't agree with you more." His dad kissed his

mom's cheek. "You stay here. I'll let you know when it's all over."

"You all better be safe out there, and bring that precious girl home." His mom took his hands. "Don't let your emotions get the better of you. Be levelheaded. Whatever Fred and Anna were thinking, they're two people with everything to lose. That makes them especially dangerous. Tamsyn is smart. I'm sure she's holding her own."

"I hope you're right, Mom." Noir tucked the weapon into his pocket. He followed his father, brothers, Eddy, and two officers out the back door.

"I have an idea," Eddy said, waving his cell.

"What's that?" Noir asked.

"We were supposed to arrest Weezer as soon as the Holiday Showcase came to an end. Fred thought it would be best if he had the honors," Eddy said.

"Fucking asshole," Noir's dad muttered.

"Here's the thing. The main room is clear. Fred's nowhere to be found. I'm going to call him. See if he answers. It would make sense for me to be looking for him. It would also make sense to be concerned that Tamsyn, and perhaps some of you, left the building."

Noir glanced to the sky. "Actually, if you told him that my parents were making a run for it, that might be amusing."

"We don't run from anything and I don't find that funny at all," his dad said.

"You both have a point. Let me call Fred. I can play

it that there's not much of a reason for me to keep you at the winery unless I'm the one who arrests you." Eddy lifted his cell to his ear as they continued down the path toward the overflow building.

Noir's heart beat in his throat. His body had gone numb, his emotions frozen in place. No anger. No fear. Just an empty, bottomless hole that couldn't be filled until Fred and Anna were caught.

And Tamsyn was back in his arms, unharmed.

"Put it on speaker," Noir said. "I want to hear his voice. I want to hear what he has to say."

"Sure thing," Eddy said. The cell rang once.

Twice.

"Eddy. What's up?" Fred answered.

"Sir, where are you? The winery is cleared. I can't ask Weezer and Carter to stay put. Unless you want me to arrest Weezer, I need you here and I can't find you anywhere. But I also can't find Weezer or Tamsyn."

Noir glanced at his father, who closed his eyes and clutched his weapon.

"Unfortunately, I saw Weezer sneak out the back. I'm following tracks through the vineyard. Stay put until I contact you. And keep the rest of the family there. Tell them I'm following a lead and will be back shortly."

"Would you like me to send someone to help?" Eddy asked.

"No. She can't be far. Looks like she's heading

toward the cottage. Probably to confront Tamsyn about something."

"Sir, that doesn't sound good. I'll send someone to—"

"Eddy. I've got it covered. Do as you're told." The line went dead.

"Jesus Christ." Eddy stuffed his cell in his pocket. "Fred has always been a pain in the ass to work for. There have been times I didn't understand his leadership and management style, but fuck. He downright lied to me." He turned. "I want you two to double-time it through the vineyard." He pointed to Merlot and Malbec. "Take cover where you can on the other side of the overflow building." He raked a hand over his head. "Carter, you're not going to like this."

"So far, I'm liking your take-charge attitude, so whatever it is, lay it on me."

"The rest of us, except Noir, are going to take cover flanking the south and the east, while Noir's going to go knock on the door," Eddy said.

"You're right. I don't like that idea." His father shook his head. "I'll do it."

"No, Dad." Noir grabbed his massive biceps. "It has to be me. Fred will shoot you on sight. He'll find a way to doctor the paperwork, making you appear to be Tamsyn's father. You'll be walking right into his plans. He can make it look like you and Tamsyn killed each other because you couldn't—"

"Yeah. Yeah. Yeah. I hear you. But you're forgetting

what that scenario could make you." His dad arched a brow.

"God, that's so disgusting, I don't even want to go there," Noir said. "But it's not me he wants. And that doesn't serve his purpose as much. He's going to be less likely to pull the trigger right away."

"Noir's right, Dad," Merlot spoke up. "I'll cover the door. I'm the best shot."

Noir shivered, remembering the time Merlot had to shoot a man holding a young mother and her baby as a shield. "Okay, just don't shoot me or my girlfriend. I plan on marrying her someday."

"Well, that's an announcement." His father cracked a smile. "Let's get this over with so my family can have some peace."

"Noir. Take this." Eddy shoved a piece of paper in his hand.

"What is it?"

"I didn't understand why Tamsyn asked me to bring it, but I do now. It's the autopsy report. It shows the necklace she was wearing."

"Thanks." Noir took the paper and stuffed it in his pocket.

"I need you to call me," Eddy said. "And leave your phone on in your pocket."

"That's a dangerous game." Noir pulled out his phone.

"I need to know what's going on so I know when to

go in. We're talking about taking down the chief of police. I can't do that on what we have so far."

"Son." His dad took him by the shoulders. "You won't have much time. I'm sure Tamsyn has done what she can to get whatever information out of him, but Fred's going to be desperate to end this in his favor. Don't give him a reason to shoot you or Tamsyn."

It was time to save the woman he loved. Never in a million years did he ever think that Tamsyn Tuttle would need saving.

Tamsyn

Tamsyn stared at Fred. She couldn't believe what he'd just told Eddy. My God, he'd lost his mind. There was no coming back from this.

"Anna, sweetheart. Go outside. I don't want you to have to see this," Fred said.

"I'm sorry, Tamsyn. I really am." Anna dug into her purse, the one she clutched to her side at all times. She handed Tamsyn a note and a document. "This will seal the Rivers' fate."

The first piece of paper had to be a forgery because it stated Carter River was her father.

The second was a note from her mother, to her, stating Carter River was her father.

Tamsyn was sure, if a handwriting expert examined it, they would state her mother hadn't written it.

"This is bullshit and again, you won't get away with it," Tamsyn said.

"You heard what Eddy said. You're missing. Weezer's nowhere in sight. It's all falling into place." Fred opened the door. He jumped. "What the fuck?"

"Surprised to see me out here?" Noir asked. "Why are you holding a gun?"

"I'm a cop. I always have a gun." Fred lowered his weapon to his side for a split second before he raised it, pointing it right at the center of Noir's chest.

Tamsyn swallowed. Her wrist exploded with a crippling pain. A guttural sob escaped her throat.

"What are you doing out here?" He stuck his head out the door before slamming it shut. "Alone?"

"Yes. I came looking for my girlfriend." He took a step toward Tamsyn, but Fred got in his way.

"We're having a family discussion. I need you to leave," Fred said.

"This is my property, so it's you who needs to leave." Noir cocked his head. "Tamsyn, are you okay?"

"I broke my wrist, but otherwise, doing just ducky." That was Tamsyn speak for having a really shitty day, and Noir knew it.

"It's cold out here," Noir said. "Why don't we all go back to the main building."

"You go ahead. I need to talk to my family first. But tell your mom and dad I need to speak to them."

"Why?" Noir asked.

"Not for you to question, son," Fred said.

"Don't ever call me son. I have a father. And I'm going to question it when you're pointing that thing at me and Tamsyn's wrist is broken. Not to mention Anna has mascara all over her face. So someone better start talking before—"

"Before what?" Fred inched closer. "Are you threatening the chief of police, because that's not going to fare well for you, especially when your mother is wanted for murder."

"That's funny."

Shit, antagonizing Fred was not going to defuse this situation. It was only going to make it worse. The last thing she wanted was for Noir to be collateral damage.

"Noir, just go," she whispered. "I have this handled."

"Fred, tell me something." Noir ignored her, and she didn't like it, but she let it go for the moment. "Now that I know everything—and I mean everything —how do you plan on disposing of me because it's one thing to set up my mom, make my dad look like Tamsyn's father, and even kill off Tamsyn, but don't you see the ripple effect here? It's too many bodies. Too many questions. State's going to—"

"Wow. Your boyfriend has quite the imagination," Anna said.

"Be quiet, Anna." Fred narrowed his stare.

"I will not." Anna stood tall.

253

"Why are you all out here anyway?" Noir asked. "Because I can't think of any other reason than to make someone disappear."

"My husband told you." She lifted her chin. "Having a family conversation. We needed a place that allowed privacy."

"My cottage would have provided that and you wouldn't have had to blow off the lock."

"If you must know," Fred said. "We wanted to warn her about your mother's arrest. We wanted to make sure she wasn't in the—"

"Are you fucking kidding me?" Tamsyn wasn't going to listen to this shit. "You've been holding a gun to me. Telling me how you're going to kill me and frame Weezer and Carter for it, and you think I'm going to stand here and let you tell this tall tale to Noir? Nope. No way. This is simple insanity if I've ever heard it."

"Oh my. You must have hit your head when you tripped," Anna said.

"Cut the crap, Anna." Fred shifted his weapon toward Tamsyn. "You're not helping, as usual."

Noir might not be a cop, but Tamsyn knew his personality well. He wasn't going to take that sitting down.

She inhaled sharply. She needed to calm the emotions before someone got killed.

Namely, her.

"There's no reason keep up the ruse. The boy knows.

And he's right. We're going to have to rethink how we play this out. It can work. We can make it look like Tamsyn and Noir uncovered the truth. They had a blowout. Yeah. Tamsyn first finds out that Weezer killed her mother."

"Anna did that and you watched," Tamsyn said.

"Not the point. It's not how history will be written." Fred had the audacity to smile.

The door burst open. Eddy and two of her other colleagues came barreling into the room.

"Drop your weapon, Fred," Eddy said. "Anna, don't you dare move."

Tamsyn raced into Noir's arms, groaning over the pain shooting through her arm. "Are you crazy? What the hell were you thinking coming in here like that? Unarmed. No backup. You could have gotten yourself killed."

He cupped her face. "And here I thought you'd be happy to see me."

"You are not going to arrest me," Fred said, hurling a few more superlatives. "I'll have your fucking badge. You have no idea what you just walked into. It was me and my wife who were being held."

"Save it, Fred." Noir pulled out a phone. "Eddy heard our entire conversation." He pulled out a gun from his other pocket. "And I wasn't unarmed. I did have backup. Not just those three cops, but my dad and three brothers are standing right behind you."

She glanced over her shoulder.

"In this family, you're never alone." He kissed her temple.

"This is bullshit. Get your fucking hands off my wife," Fred protested.

"I want them off my property," Carter said.

"It will be my pleasure." Eddy cuffed the chief of police. The man who took her in.

Her father.

Jesus, what a shitshow.

"Come on." Noir wrapped his arm around her waist. "We better get that X-rayed."

"I guess I should say thank you." She rested her head on his strong shoulder. "I honestly thought he was going to kill me."

He kissed her temple. "Unfortunately, we all thought that. But it's over. He and Anna are going to go away for a long time."

"Hey, Tamsyn." Carter stepped in their path. "I'm so sorry, about everything. I should have—"

"You couldn't have known." She eased from Noir's warm embrace and hugged Carter. "I lived with him for years and had no idea. I never even suspected, so how could you have? I appreciate everything you've done for me—and my mother—over the years. You've been more like a father to me than anyone."

"I'll settle for being a father-in-law someday." He squeezed her shoulders.

"That's putting the cart before the horse." She felt the heat rush to her cheeks.

"Not according to my—"

"That's enough, Dad. I need to get Tamsyn to urgent care. Then I'm sure she'll be needed at the station for a statement."

"You all will be," Eddy said as he dragged Fred down the path, still kicking and screaming.

"We're going to need a new chief. That's going to suck," she mumbled.

"I know who I want to back," Carter said. "She's perfect for the job."

"I couldn't agree more." Eddy smiled.

Tamsyn couldn't believe her ears. It wasn't something she ever thought about. Not seriously anyway. Fred had mentioned it a time or two, but it wasn't something she thought about. Finding her mother's killer was more important than advancing her career.

However, now that Fred had disappointed her on so many levels, the idea eased into her brain like a bright light. Not because Fred had thought she was capable, but because Fred had used it to control her in many ways, like he'd done her entire life. He dangled it over her head like a carrot. So many things made sense now.

But what mattered most was she had answers. They weren't the ones she wanted. However, the secrets of her life had been unraveled. It was time to stop living in the past and look to the future.

"Noir," she whispered.

"Yes?"

"I love you."

"I know," he said. "I love you back."

"What your dad said, about being a father-in-law. I wouldn't mind that."

Noir stopped in the middle of the path.

His dad chuckled. His brothers laughed, slapping Noir on the back as they passed.

"Are you proposing to me, Tamsyn Tuttle?"

"Absolutely not." She smiled. "But I'm giving you permission to do it right."

16

NOIR

SIX WEEKS LATER...

Noir took Tamsyn's hand. It had been an emotional roller coaster the last few weeks.

The worst had been Fred's decision to take his own life.

Anna had gone from claiming innocence to being forced to go along with Fred's diabolical plan, to now possibly going for an insanity plea.

The trial was going to be a shitshow.

The reporters were relentless, especially Alison. She didn't seem to care who she hurt to get her story.

"Are you okay?" he asked. "Today was a long day."

"I'm just glad Anna won't be getting out anytime soon. But the woman isn't insane. Not by the truest definition of the word."

He palmed her cheek. "No. She's not. I wish I could tell you that it is all over. But I can tell you that it's all going to work out. They can't hurt you anymore."

"Your family has been so amazing. I don't know what I'd do without them."

"They all feel the same way about you." He arched a brow. "They will feel safer knowing you're the new chief of police."

She rolled her eyes. "I still can't believe that one. I'm the youngest in the history of this town."

"You're going to be the best."

"I appreciate it. I just better not be turning the other way when my boyfriend or his family gets parking tickets in this town."

He chuckled. "Only Zinny avoids that rule." He brushed the hair from her face. "It's Merlot's lead foot you should be concerned about."

"Your family is a little bit nuts, but I'm falling just as much in love with them as I love you."

"That's sweet." He brushed his lips across her mouth. Could this be the right time? No. It wasn't the right place. He should wait until they were back at the cottage. Or maybe next week when they moved into Dax and Chablis' garage apartment.

Better yet, he should take her on a romantic overnight. Maybe to Cape May.

"I love you, Tamsyn. My family does too. You've always got a place here with us." He held her gaze for a long, awkward moment. The ring burned a hole in his pocket. He'd been carrying it around for five days. Once, he thought he'd lost it.

His heart hammered in his chest. He dug his hand

into his pocket and fingered the diamond. It wasn't very big or flashy. But Tamsyn wouldn't have wanted anything too showy. She was a simple girl with simple desires.

His father strolled into the den carrying two glasses of wine. "I'm so sorry to interrupt. Your mother sent me with these. She thought the two of you could use a little relaxation." He glanced toward Tamsyn's left hand and scowled. For the last week, all anyone ever did was look at her freaking ring finger.

He regretted telling any of them he'd bought a ring. It's all they thought about.

However, he wasn't sure this was the right time.

Her biological father had just died. The woman who raised her was facing life in prison. Tamsyn's world had been turned upside down. It didn't matter that there was a lot of good going on too. He needed to pick the perfect time.

"Thanks, Dad." He sipped his wine.

Tamsyn shook her head. "Thanks, but I'll pass."

"We're all going to be eating apple crumble. Trey and Ashling made it. I can tell you it's delicious. When you're done in here, come join us."

"We will," Tamsyn said.

"I'm starving." Noir couldn't do this here. Other family members had made big productions and proposed in front of everyone. That wasn't Noir. He was quiet. Private. He'd do it at home.

If he ever got up the courage.

"This is getting ridiculous." Tamsyn took his glass from his hand and handed it back to Carter. "Your son is a chickenshit."

"I'm well aware." Carter laughed. "If you really want to call him out, haul his ass into the family room. All his siblings, their spouses, nieces and nephews, and his mother are there."

"Sounds like a plan." She yanked him by the elbow.

"What the heck? What is going on?" He tripped over his own two feet as Tamsyn marched him through the hallway and into the family room where everyone sat in front of the fireplace. It was a cold January day. The snow was piling up outside and shortly, once all the babies went down, everyone planned on going outside, building snowmen, and having a snowball fight.

Good River family fun.

"He still hasn't done it?" His mother lifted her gaze from her cross-stitch.

"Nope." Tamsyn dug her hand into his pocket.

"Hey. Stop that." He tried batting her hand away, but she was too fast.

She pulled out the diamond.

Everyone busted out laughing.

"Do you have something you want to ask me? Or shall I just put this on my finger and start planning our wedding with your mother? Personally, I don't want to wait too long. So, if it's okay with all of you, I'd like to do it in a couple of weeks. I know weddings have been done at the winery, but considering my family history here, I'm thinking maybe we do a small ceremony in the park. Justice of the peace? Sound good to you?"

Noir blinked. He swallowed. He opened his mouth but no words escaped his lips. He cleared his throat and tried again. "Oh hell. Tamsyn, I love you. Do you want to get married?"

"I think my answer was clear." She wiggled her finger with the diamond on it. She wrapped her arms around Noir. "I love you, but you suck at hiding things. I've known about that ring since you bought it."

"I can't keep anything from a cop."

"Not any cop. The chief of police." She smiled. "I love you."

"I love you too," he said, heat rising to his cheeks as his entire family made a collective *aww*.

With the exception of Ashling and TJ. They both said in unison *gross, get a room*.

"Now that I have all of you in one room," Tamsyn said. "I do have a different kind of announcement." She took Noir's hand and placed it on her stomach.

"Oh my God." His mother jumped from her chair, tossing her cross-stitch to the ground.

"Are you okay, Mom?" Noir asked.

"You should be asking your fiancée that." His mom took Tamsyn into her arms and hugged her tight.

"Well, I'll be damned," his dad said. "I'm going to start losing count of all these grandkids."

"Grandkids?" Noir took a step back and raked a

hand across the top of his head. He stared at Tamsyn, who swiped at her cheeks. "Are you pregnant?"

"That's right. You're going to be a daddy. That's why I couldn't stand around and wait for you to figure out when the perfect time would be to propose. I needed you to just get it over with so we could get on with it."

"I need to sit down." But instead, Noir took Tamsyn into his arms and twirled her around. He'd finally found his perfect match.

EPILOGUE
CARTER

One Year Later...

C arter held Elizabeth Weezer River in his arms. She held his thumb with a death grip as she smiled and cooed while he made a funny face. She was a feisty, fiery little girl. Born a few weeks early, but healthy and with a set of lungs that rocked the world. She was a good mix of both families. She had her mother's eyes and her father's soul. She was the new heartbeat of the family home and Carter couldn't be happier about his decision to give the house to his son and his family.

He stared at the crackling fire. His other grandchildren, the lot of them, played at his feet while his wife sat on the floor, smiling and laughing. His children and

JEN TALTY

their spouses were all present. Even Corbin, his oldest grandchild, had managed to come home for New Year's.

He swiped at his cheek.

"Are you crying, old man?" Weezer tapped his knee.

"I most certainly am not."

Noir laughed. "Between my daughter, Nebbiolo's son, and Zinny being pregnant again, he's an emotional wreck."

"He gets all teary-eyed every time I walk into the house," Corbin added. "Asking me what day I leave."

"I was helping your grandma chop onions this morning for her famous omelets." Carter hated to admit his family was right. He'd spent a lifetime doing his best to protect his wife. His kids. And their spouses. His life hadn't been easy. It had been riddled with lies, manipulations, buried secrets, and pains of the past that could have destroyed each and every member of his family. It had taken a world of hurt to get them to this point.

It was hard not to wait for the other shoe to drop.

But for the first time in his sixty-plus years on this earth, he's spent an entire year with no drama.

Okay, that wasn't entirely true.

Weezer had still cheated to win the Holiday Showcase. However, this time the whole town stood back and let it happen.

And everyone pulled together to make it the best showcase this community had ever seen.

For the first time in years, no one was trying to take something from the River family. There were no secrets hanging over their heads. Nothing buried in the vineyard to be unearthed. No one gunning for their destruction.

They had peace to be a family. To love one another. To walk through town with their heads held high, and the only whispers or gossip was that of old stories that made people laugh.

"Grandpa," TJ said. "Aren't you the one who always tells me that showing emotion is a good thing and that if we let it stay bottled up, it will come out sideways and at the wrong time?" He inched closer to Weezer, helping with one of the smaller children. TJ was good like that. God, that boy had grown so much in the last year. He was almost six feet tall. His hockey playing skills had exploded. He was on the starting line. He thrived under Dax's coaching. But what really made that boy come out of his shell had been being adopted by Zinny.

What a proud moment that had been for the entire family.

It was hard to believe that TJ could be leaving for Juniors up in Canada come September. That would be both exciting and sad for Carter. TJ might not be biologically a River, but Carter loved that boy like his own flesh and blood.

More tears filled Carter's eyes. This holiday season had been both the easiest and the hardest. But only hard because Carter had realized he didn't know how to handle life without conflict. He'd dreamed of it. Hoped for it. Even prayed for it. Now that he had it, he cherished it. He honestly did. He just didn't know how to live in it day in and day out.

"Your grandfather is turning to an old softy." Weezer smiled. "I'm liking this new version, except now he's threatening to retire. He doesn't have enough hobbies in order to do that."

"Maybe I'll take up golf," he said.

Malbec laughed. "Why don't you join the gun club with Silas? And we can always use good babysitters."

Elizabeth wiggled in his arms. Her little arms flapped. Her big blue eyes squinted, and her lips quivered.

"I think this little girl is getting hungry," Carter said. "As soon as I finish these last few cases I'm working on, I will be officially retired, and I was thinking that your mother and I would take a trip to Europe this spring. For like a month. She's never been."

"But I'm not retiring." Weezer glared.

"Oh, yes, you are," Merlot said. "We can handle the winery. You don't work that much anymore as it is."

"Not the point," Weezer said. "Besides, you all still come to me for advice."

"We can still do that," Eliza Jane said.

"She's right." Noir lifted his fussy daughter from Carter's arms. "We always have you close if we need you. It's not like we want you out. But you and Dad deserve to enjoy the years you have left."

"I agree." Nebbiolo held his little boy like a pro. He was a natural at being a father, something that honestly shocked Carter. Nebbiolo hadn't been the most mature kid, or adult. But June had changed all that in a flash.

"This feels like you kids are trying to get rid of us," Weezer said.

"Not at all, Mom." Chablis moved to the floor, wrapping her arm around her mother. "You and Dad are still so young. You raised seven kids. It's our turn to take care of things. If we need help, we're not going to be shy about asking."

"We're all so appreciative of everything you've done for us," Riesling said. "I might not work for the winery, but I do help out when and where I can. We want to see you and Dad enjoy your golden years while you're still young enough to do it."

"I agree with our kids." Carter stood, taking his wife's hand, helping her up. "Now, let's get some of these dishes done and clean up this house before we head back to the cottage."

"Nope. Not going to let you do that," Tamsyn said. "Noir and I can handle that."

"But we made a huge mess and holidays are a lot with this family," Weezer said. "It's always in the main house and I feel bad that it's now left to the two of you to deal with."

"You gave us this house. We willingly took on what that meant." Noir kissed his mother's cheek.

"We will help them," Zinny said. "You and Dad should go home and have a nightcap. Watch some TV. Get a little frisky."

"Gross," Ashling said. "Grandparents don't do that."

Carter laughed. "Let's hope your grandma and I are—"

"Dad." Riesling patted his shoulder. "Seriously. We don't need to get into that conversation."

"I know what sex is, Mom." Ashling planted her hands on her hips. "It's just weird that old people do it."

"Watch who you call old, young lady." Weezer ruffled Ashling's hair. "Come on, old man, let's go make Weezer noises."

"Oh my God," TJ said. "I can't believe my teenage ears have been subjected to this. It's worse than when Tommy Sisco brought one of his aunt's romance novels and read the sex scene in the locker room."

"He did what?" Dax asked. "How come this is the first I'm hearing of this?"

The room boomed with laughter.

Carter smiled. His heart filled with the kind of joy that couldn't be explained. This was exactly what he pictured his life to be the day he married Weezer. He knew she would bring him the kind of life that fed his soul. "You all have a good night." He guided his wife to the front of the house. He helped her into her jacket before putting on his own.

The cold January evening hit his old bones, but he still wasn't tired of changing seasons. It reminded him of the life he'd lived so far, and he looked forward to the next chapter.

He threaded his fingers through Weezer's as they strolled down the path toward the cottage. "We did good, Weezer."

She leaned in closer. "Our children have found the kind of happiness we have, only they don't have the pains of the past to suffer through like we did. I'm so grateful to you for sticking by me all these years." She glanced up. Tears dribbled down her face.

He rubbed them away with his thumb.

"You didn't have to. When I divorced you, a lesser man would have called it quits."

"I've loved you my whole life. There isn't another woman for me. Secrets or no secrets. I couldn't have stopped loving you if I tried."

"Do you really want to take me to Europe?"

"I do." He paused, taking her into his arms. He glanced between the cottage and what used to be his home. "It's time to turn everything over to the kids. While they will always need us in some way, whether it be to watch the grandbabies or to be there for moral support, they don't need us to hover anymore. You taught them the business. They know what they are doing. They each have a family to love and call their own. It's time for us to do the one thing we've never done."

"Travel?"

"That, and just be us. We'd only been married a few years before we started pumping out kids. But we never got to be Carter and Weezer. There's always been something standing in our way. Not our kids, but life and our need to protect our family from the past. We don't have to do that anymore. We can relax and simply be us."

"I like the sound of that."

Carter pressed his lips against his wife's.

His family was safe and secure.

Life at The River Winery was finally the way it was supposed to be. Filled with love, laughter, and family.

Thank you for taking the time to read A LITTLE BIT WHISKEY. I have enjoyed sharing the River family with you. Please feel free to leave an honest review!

HAVE WE GOT A STORY FOR YOU!

Dear Readers:

Welcome to Candlewood Falls!

Each Candlewood Falls story stands alone. However, the end of one story doesn't mean the end of your favorite characters. They can show up in any Candlewood Falls book at any time.

Candlewood Falls is a unique world of connected stories by different authors whose characters, business, and events appear in each others' stories.

Think of Candlewood Falls as a literary soap opera.

Be sure to check out the the other authors and discover which other books include your favorite characters.

Happy reading!

Stacey Wilk & K.M Fawcett & Jen Talty

READY FOR ANOTHER TRIP TO CANDLEWOOD FALLS?

I'm super excited about the rest of the River Family and their stories. Check these out by moi - Jen Talty *USA Today* Bestselling Author

There was one problem that stood in his way...and he was falling in love with her. ***Rivers Edge***

Some truths weren't meant to be uncovered. THE BURIED SECRET

Where broken dreams collide, two hearts will come together and find the love they thought they lost. ITS IN HIS KISS

She was only supposed to help with his sone...only she showed him what family and love was truly about. LIPS OF AN ANGEL

He's not prepared for what the past is about to unearth, or the danger it will bring to a family he didn't know he had. ***Kisses Sweeter than Wine***

For more Alpachino the Alpaca antics and to find out who went to prison for killing Sam's Father's read <u>TAKING ROOT</u> by Stacey Wilk.

And the second book in Stacey's series…What will Brad Wilde the man who has it all do when an orphan is dropped on his doorstep? RAISING WINTER by Stacey Wilk.

Also by Stacey Wilk in this series: Even the most unexpected circumstances may teach us how to forgive what cannot be changed. DEFINING CHANCES.

And While packing away her mothers life, Petra Wilde discovers a life of her own in BEGINNING OVER.

If you want to spend some time with Sam Wilde and his quest for an apple to make you happy and horny you'll want to read WILDE TEMPTATION by K.M. FAWCETT.

And the second book in K.M. Fawcett's series…Spend the holidays with Lacey Wilde, her dog Remi, and a sexy marine who claims Remi belongs to him in <u>WILDE CHRISTMAS</u> by K.M. Fawcett.

Also by K.M. Fawcett is WILD IN LOVE: Can a bad boy and a good girl overcome their fears to find true love?

And in WILDE TREASURES: While searching for a hidden fortune, can two lonely adventurers discover some treasurers are more precious than gold.

Thank you for visiting Candlewood Falls!

Be sure to leave a review to help readers like you
find and enjoy our small town.

Join our exciting community of authors and readers at the
Candlewood Falls Facebook Readers Group for cover reveals,
sneak peaks, deleted scenes, and excerpts from upcoming
releases. Plus games and fun!

ACKNOWLEDGMENTS

A big thank you to Stacey Wilk and K.M. Fawcett for inviting me into Candlewood Falls.

ABOUT THE AUTHOR

Jen Talty is the *USA Today* Bestselling Author of Contemporary Romance, Romantic Suspense, and Paranormal Romance. In the fall of 2020, her short story was selected and featured in a 1001 Dark Nights Anthology.

Regardless of the genre, her goal is to take you on a ride that will leave you floating under the sun with warmth in your heart. She writes stories about broken heroes and heroines who aren't necessarily looking for romance, but in the end, they find the kind of love books are written about :).

She first started writing while carting her kids to one hockey rink after the other, averaging 170 games per year between 3 kids in 2 countries and 5 states. Her first book, IN TWO WEEKS was originally published in 2007. In 2010 she helped form a publishing company (Cool Gus Publishing) with *NY Times* Bestselling Author Bob Mayer where she ran the technical side of the business through 2016.

Jen is currently enjoying the next phase of her life...the empty nester! She and her husband reside in Jupiter, Florida.

Grab a glass of vino, kick back, relax, and let the romance roll in...

Sign up for my _Newsletter (https://dl.bookfunnel.com/82gm8b9k4y)_ where I often give away free books before publication.

Join my private _Facebook group_ (https://www.facebook.com/groups/191706547909047/) where I post exclusive excerpts and discuss all things murder and love!

And on Bookbub: bookbub.com/authors/jen-talty

- facebook.com/AuthorJenTalty
- instagram.com/jen_talty
- bookbub.com/authors/jen-talty
- amazon.com/author/jentalty
- pinterest.com/jentalty

ALSO BY JEN TALTY

Brand new series: SAFE HARBOR!

Mine To Keep

Mine To Save

Mine To Protect

Mine to Hold

Mine to Love

Check out LOVE IN THE ADIRONDACKS!

Shattered Dreams

An Inconvenient Flame

The Wedding Driver

Clear Blue Sky

Blue Moon

Before the Storm

NY STATE TROOPER SERIES (also set in the Adirondacks!)

In Two Weeks

Dark Water

Deadly Secrets

Murder in Paradise Bay

To Protect His own

Cove's Blind Date Blows Up

My Everyday Hero – Ledger

Tempting Tavor

Malachi's Mystic Assignment

Needing Neor

Holiday Romances

A Christmas Getaway

Alaskan Christmas

Whispers

Christmas In The Sand

Heroes & Heroines on the Field

Taking A Risk

Tee Time

A New Dawn

The Blind Date

Spring Fling

Summers Gone

Winter Wedding

The Awakening

The Collective Order

The Lost Sister

The Lost Soldier

The Lost Soul

The Lost Connection

The New Order